MAID IN MANHATTAN

By the same author

Panic Room

MAID IN MANHATTAN

A Novel by James Ellison
Based on the Motion Picture
Story by Edmond Dantes
Screenplay Written by Kevin Wade

ROBERT HALE · LONDON

ISBN 0 7090 7516 2

Robert Hale Limited
Clerkenwell House
Clerkenwell Green
London EC1R 0HT

2 4 6 8 10 9 7 5 3 1

Typeset in 11/16½ Aldine
by Derek Doyle & Associates, Liverpool.
Printed in Great Britain by
St Edmundsbury Press, Bury St Edmunds, Suffolk.
Bound by Woolnough Bookbinding Ltd.

1

Marisa Ventura had no idea on this particular weekend in the early fall that her life was about to undergo a major change. An unselfconscious, consummate beauty in her late twenties, she divided her working days between two totally different worlds. There was the New York City of boutiques and boites and beautifully dressed people, most of them sculpted and slender, where she toiled as a maid in the Beresford Hotel in midtown Manhattan. And then there was the Bronx of bodegas, OTB parlors, street corner pushers and users, drunks and three-card Monte dealers accompanied by a constant symphony of ambulance and police sirens. This was the world where she lived, in a cramped one-bedroom box, and brought up her ten-year-old son, Ty. She prided herself on her inner strength, and managed to reconcile these two worlds with neither envy nor regret. Her job paid the bills with enough left over to buy books for Ty, an omnivorous reader. A gifted six-grader who could easily ace eighth-grade work according to his homeroom teacher, Ty was the apple of his mother's eye, the pride of her life. Where does it come from? she often asked herself.

Those smarts of his. I'm OK, certainly no rocket scientist but I can read the *Times* without moving my lips, and Marcus, she reflected, was smart enough, although he rarely used it. He was mentally lazy and relied on guile and a kind of male bombastic charm to get him through life.

Marisa and Marcus had been high school sweethearts and she became pregnant soon after graduation. Marcus was of Irish-American background, a well-intended guy who never followed through on his commitments. Ty's birth was a joyous event for Marisa but one that began the rapid decline of her relationship with Marcus, who was more interested in the next party than the next paycheck. After draining Marisa's savings, she told him to get lost and decided to raise Ty on her own.

By the time Ty was two years old, it was clear that Marisa and Marcus had spawned a gifted child, perhaps a genius. He spoke fluently, he could read, he knew his ABCs, and all of his colors. He was a spontaneous and endless question-asking machine.

That was eight years ago. Marcus continued seeing Ty on some weekends and special occasions, but he had a habit of disappointing the boy by breaking dates at the last moment.

On a Friday morning in early autumn, Marisa was going through her usual morning routine with Ty, which consisted mainly of trying to move him from square one to square two so that he wouldn't be late for school. Ty was not a morning person and tended to move at a snail's pace. He was wearing headphones as he slowly laced up his sneakers, while Marisa packed his well-worn duffel bag with clothes, books and CDs. After school he was going on a camping weekend with his father.

'You sure you don't want some breakfast, honey?' she said.

He didn't hear her. She slipped off his headphones and repeated the question.

'I'm not hungry.'

'Breakfast is supposed to be the most important meal of the day,' she told him, not for the first time. 'You know, the healthiest.'

'Sorry, Ma. It holds no appeal for me.'

She held up four thick books. 'You really want to bring these?'

'Huh?' He was concentrating on a recalcitrant double knot in his left sneaker, which persisted in not lacing no matter how much he fiddled with it. Manual dexterity was not one of Ty's strong points; he preferred to inhabit the large spaces of his mind.

'I said do I have to pack all these?'

He glanced up and took a book from her. 'This is really good, Ma. Living history. It puts you in touch with the way politics work.'

She took the book back from him and read the title, shaking her head. '*Abuse of Power: The New Nixon Tapes*. C'mon, Ty. You're going camping with your dad, not to some think tank.'

He rose from the side of the bed and attacked a messy pile of papers, tapes, CDs and assorted junk that he collected and refused to throw away until he fished out a favorite game boy.

'Here,' he said. 'This goes in.' He concentrated again on his left sneaker. Finally wrestling the knot into at least approximate tightness, he looked up at his mother with a smile. 'Did you know Paul Simon wrote "American Tune" as a reaction to Nixon's election?'

'No, I didn't know that.' She studied her son with a fond smile, then said, 'You taking the puzzles?'

'No way. They annoy dad.'

'OK.'

'He was pissed off. The definition of American didn't include everyone who came to this country.'

'Your father is often pissed off.'

'I know. He cares deeply about things. But I meant Paul, not dad. He was singing for us, you know? You, me, Abuela, her parents, their parents. . . . For the poor, the dispossessed. For everyone.'

'We'll have to thank Mr Simon,' Marisa said dryly. 'Come on, Ty. The shoe is *tied* now. Leave it alone. We're going to be late.'

When they finally left the apartment, Marisa walked three steps ahead of her son, hoping that would hurry him along. They had two blocks to walk to the corner where they would catch the MTA bus. Ty's headphones were once more in place and he slumped like a little old man under the weight of his backpack. Marisa carried the duffel bag.

'You want to do your speech for me?'

He was oblivious.

'Ty!' she shouted. 'Hel*lo*?' She removed his headphones and music bled out into the autumn air. 'Now maybe you can hear me. Why don't you turn that off?'

'It's Simon and Garfunkel.'

'Oh sorry. I didn't know.'

'You can't just turn them off, not in the middle of a song,' he said, absently admonishing her. 'It's insulting. They deserve better than that.'

'I understand.'

She steered him toward the line at the bus stop. 'Careful – watch that puddle.'

Ty was often at least one remove from his surroundings and she was still terrified when he crossed heavily trafficked streets by himself.

'Why did they break up?' he said.

'Who?'

'Simon and Garfunkel.'

'You got me. Don't have a clue. You can Google it at school.'

As they waited for the bus to come she stared at her son. Sometimes she found it hard to believe that she and Marcus had produced this strange and wonderful child. So gentle, so brilliant. A hopeless slob, dangerously absent-minded, endearing and totally honest. She said, 'Everything's got its own time, Ty. Then the time's up. This is true with everything, you know what I'm saying?'

Ty nodded and gave her a squirrelly, thoughtful look. 'You mean like you and dad? I imagine there was a time when you guys were right.'

She smiled at him, wondering how she would ever be able to figure out this wacko kid, whose mind raced like a finely tuned motor.

'Yeah,' she said. 'Sure there was a time like that. C'mon – stay up with me. You're straggling. . . .'

When they reached the bus stop, Ty said, 'Ma – important question.'

'Hmmm?'

'Pause and think before you answer, OK?'

'OK. *What*?'

'I'm just wondering what would happen if I didn't give the speech today.'

9

The bus arrived with a belch of dark exhaust and Ty boarded first, showing the driver his student pass. Marisa swiped her metro card.

'You're used up, lady,' the bus driver said.

She frowned at him. 'Excuse me?'

'He means your metro card, Ma.'

'Oh.' She began fishing in her handbag for change.

'Damn it,' she muttered, 'I knew it was out of rides. Ty – you got any change?'

He dug in his pockets as she extracted coins from the bottom of her bag and dropped them into the bin. 'One thirty-five, one forty, one forty-five. . . .' Ty fished out a Red Cross knife but no coins.

A line was forming behind her, and the bus driver, staring fixedly through the windshield, was whistling impatiently. Digging further, she finally found a nickel. 'OK, one-fifty. Sorry. Come on, Ty, move it.'

The front of the bus was packed, and as they slid into seats in the back row, Ty said, 'About the speech. . . .'

'Yes, as you were saying. What *about* the speech?'

'Now don't get angry.'

'I think I'm already getting angry.'

'Would I get in trouble if I decided not to give it?'

'You'd get in trouble with me and your father.'

'I'm not really feeling it, Ma. It's just not there for me. Every time I think about it, about standing up there and giving it, I feel really crummy.'

She knocked on his head with her knuckles. 'What's goin' on in there? You worked all summer on that speech. *All summer*, Ty. I can't wait to hear it – and believe me, I'm going to hear it.'

Ty sank down in his seat. 'It's boring, it's dry, it's dead. I hate it, and my reputation at school will only sink lower. If that's possible.'

'Well, the speech is not boring to me, or to Abuela, or your dad. So you just may be wrong about that.'

'I thought we were meeting dad afterwards.'

'No way,' she said, a sharp note creeping into her tone. 'He's coming. He'll be there. Then you go camping. That's why I'm hauling this duffel bag, giving myself a hernia.'

'Can women get hernias?'

'I don't know. I think so.' She glanced at her son and absently brushed lint off his jacket. 'What's wrong, honey?'

'You know dad's going to be late,' he said quietly. 'If he shows up at all. Everyone will see him come in late. It would be better if he just didn't come.'

'He knows what time it starts, Ty. Don't worry. He wouldn't miss this for the world.'

Ty nodded. His features were still knotted with worry as he put his headphones back on. She studied him for a moment before reaching over and lifting them from his head. 'Hey – look at me a second.'

'What?'

'You got something on your face.'

She leaned close to wipe it off, then kissed him instead. She laughed and said, 'You're some smart kid, Ty, they don't come any smarter. But you always fall for it, don't you?'

'I guess I do.' He wiggled away from her and added, 'I wish you'd stop it, Ma. It's embarrassing. I'm getting too old for that mushy stuff.'

'I sincerely hope not,' she said.

★

11

Ty's school was a grim old pile of red brick, condemned thirty years ago, then unaccountably kept open for new generations of students to deface. Ty had already skipped one grade, and was the youngest and one of the smallest in his class. He was known as The Brain and Brainiac, and among his peers these were terms of opprobrium on a par with faggot and locker thief. Marisa felt protective of him; he was a babe in the woods in this public school Bronx jungle.

'Jesus,' she said, staring at a tall girl in tight yellow slacks and a blouse that left her navel and many inches of her midriff exposed. She was thirteen but was made up to look older. 'Is that Tiana Zatkowsky? Wow, she's had a growth spurt.'

Ty was looking around with his myopic squint. His mother nudged him. 'She's walking right over there. Are you gonna tutor her again this year?'

They caught up to the girl and she smiled sweetly at Ty. 'Hey, little man. 'Sup?'

' 'Sup with you?' he said with all the cool he could muster.

'Wanna walk to assembly?'

'Sure, OK.' He started to walk away, casually ignoring his mother, then at the last moment turned to her and said, 'The speech thing – it starts at—'

'I know, I know,' she interrupted, smiling. 'C'mere, Ty. You got something on your face.'

He backed away and raised his hand. 'Oh no. Not twice in one day. I'm not that stupid.'

'OK, honey. Have a good day. I love you.'

'Love you,' he said in a whisper.

She watched him walk off with Tiana as a black sedan pulled up to the curb. Assemblyman Christopher Marshall stepped out of the car followed by his chief of staff Jerry Seigal. The two men, a study in contrasts, were deep in conversation. Where Marshall was tall, slender and fair complected, a perfect model of the ideal WASP, Seigal was short, dark and practically bald. Where Marshall spoke slowly and with an impeccable educated eastern accent, Seigal spoke with a rat-a-tat-tat delivery as though perpetually stoked on caffeine. Both men were in their middle thirties; they formed a successful team, with Marshall charming the public and Seigal, as loyal to him as a lapdog to his master, constantly maneuvering behind the scenes, always looking for the edge. He secretly hoped that one day, perhaps fifteen or twenty years down the line, Chris Marshall would be elected president of the United States. Seigal would then be the power behind the throne, the human lock box containing all the secrets, deals, lies and broken promises it takes to reach the top.

Marisa Ventura and Christopher Marshall passed by one another, both of them preoccupied by their own scheduled lives. Marisa, glancing at him, thought, What a hunk. But he's a politician. That was her way of automatically dismissing him as a person of any intrinsic worth. She had been conditioned by Marcus since high school to judge all politicians, regardless of party or professed platforms, as phonies and sell outs, interested only in their own self-aggrandizement.

Marshall cut through something Seigal was saying. 'No, no. Don't make too much out of this, Jerry. Until I announce, this is just a fact-finding tour. Don't turn it into a campaign.'

As they continued walking toward the school entrance, kids turned to stare at them. There was a buzz in the air.

These middle school Bronx children were not accustomed to seeing well-dressed white men like Christopher Marshall visiting their school. Ty and Tiana were among those watching the two men as they walked slowly, continuing to converse.

'It's all a campaign, buddy,' Seigal insisted. 'You know that. You think anyone gives a shit about announcements? Your whole life is one campaign.'

'Enough,' Marshall said. 'Drop it.'

Tiana whispered to Ty, 'That's one studly dude.'

'He's an assemblyman,' Ty said. 'He has a very good voting record.' He cocked his head and stared at the two men. 'I guess he's slumming in our neighborhood.'

'Have you ever seen such blue eyes?' Tiana said. 'Just like the sky.'

'The sky is overcast,' Ty pointed out.

'Oh you know what I mean, stupid.'

Seigal leaned closer to Marshall and said, 'People know you're gonna run for your old man's seat, and they love it, they eat it up. It's like a fairy story.' Seigal's head quickly swiveled. 'Hey, look at that!'

A horde of photographers and press were standing near the school entrance, poised to descend on Marshall.

'You see what I'm saying?' Seigal raced on. 'A little press for the school and some juicy press for the future Senator from the great state of New York.'

Microphones and cameras were shoved into Marshall's face. He forced himself to smile. The school's principal rushed through the door, his tie flying over his shoulder, and grasped Marshall's hand.

'Mr Marshall,' he said breathlessly, 'Carlos Valesquez, the

principal. May I say how sorry I am about your father's passing. Speaking for our middle school, I offer our heartfelt sympathy.'

'Thank you, Mr Valesquez.'

Jerry Seigal pushed up close to Valesquez and said, 'Hey, school principal, how about a picture? You and the assemblyman shaking hands. Yeah – big smile. Great!'

The cameras snapped away, and Ty, in the distance, stood seeming to take it all in, but his mind was elsewhere.

'I just hope dad comes on time,' he muttered under his breath. 'Just don't screw up, OK?'

2

The two leading tabloids that morning featured stories and front-line photos of Assemblyman Christopher Marshall arguing with a beautiful blond on a Manhattan street corner. The headline of one of the tabloids read: CHRIS MARSHALLING HIS DEFENSES, with this sub-headline: **Son of late senator Grant Marshall calls off engagement to super model!**

Many of the riders on the subway Marisa took into the city had their noses buried in the sensational doings of Marshall, but Marisa's own nose was buried in *The Drama of the Gifted Child*, as she held onto a ceiling strap with one hand. Marcus believed that newspapers and most of the media were either reductive, or self-glorifying, or tools of the power elite, or sometimes all three. Although Marisa knew that he exaggerated, as he was prone to do about almost everything, she preferred books to magazines and newspapers. She felt they had lasting value, unlike newspapers, which served up the same old trivia and repeat stories as a daily supplement to your coffee and Danish. She had also developed a powerful motivation to self educate herself.

How else could she ever hope to stay up with Ty?

Her stop was Fiftieth Street on the 6 local. She expertly navigated the crowd and raced up the stairs. As she walked two blocks south and one block west to the Beresford Hotel, she punched at her cell phone. 'Marcus – it's me. Listen up now, Ty's speech starts at four and *you cannot be late.* I mean it. 'Bye.'

As she entered the richly carpeted entrance to the Beresford she spotted Cora, a well-dressed sales girl who worked at the posh jewelry store inside the spacious lobby.

' 'Sup, Cora?' Marisa said with a grin. 'How my diamonds doin'?'

'They're laid away with your rubies and your emeralds.'

'I'll be by for them one of these days.'

'Should I hold my breath?'

'Better not, girl. It might not be good for your health.'

Marisa continued past a bank of telephone operators working the phones. Irene, one of the operators, winked at Marisa as she said into the phone in her practiced, haughty tones, 'Beresford. One moment please. . . .'

'Always put 'em on hold,' Marisa said, grinning. 'Makes us sound busy.'

She rounded the corner, took the service entrance and rushed up to the Beresford security desk. Keef Townsend, an elderly African American, was sitting at his bank of monitors as Marisa reached for her time card on the wall.

'Good morning, Marisa,' Keef said, looking up with a smile. His voice was kindly and deep.

' 'Sup, Keef?' She swiped her card through. 'Just on time.'

'You always on time. Never seen you to be late.'

'Yeah, sure. I'm perfect, Keef, right?'

'Right as rain,' he said. 'And speakin' of the weather, how does it look for today?'

It was the same question he asked her every day, and she would have felt deprived to start the morning without it. 'Some sun, some clouds,' she said. 'Real nice.'

'Ah, that sound real nice.'

She glanced at the monitors. 'Anything good on? Some juicy action to get me into the swing of things?'

He punched a dial and gestured to her, and she saw, in grainy black and white, a stocky middle-aged man frantically pounding on a room door. He was completely naked and his sagging buttocks quivered as he pressed himself up against the door and pounded on it. His free hand was covering his privates with a newspaper.

'He opened the door to fetch the *Times*,' Keef said in his melodious North Carolina accent. 'The wife, she just pushed him on out.'

Marisa shook her head and winced. 'Damn – that nasty ole butt first thing in the morning. I'd kick him out, too. Oh wait, hold on – I know the guy – he's one of mine. The lactose intolerant.'

'I like how you name people, Marisa. Hair curler lady. Mister accidentally-on-purpose-expose-himself. I wonder what you call me behind my back.'

'Clark Gable,' she said as she picked up the house phone and dialed. 'We need a robe to the Charles Suite ASAP.' She turned to Keef with a grin. 'Only kidding. What I call you is God. Because you see it all and you still smile.'

Keef nodded, pleased. 'I cool with that. I surely am.'

'See ya later, God.'

'See ya, Marisa.'

She headed down a long service stairway, passing underneath leaking heating pipes and passing dumpsters loaded with garbage and a maintenance team doing repairs. The smells were dank and heavy. The belly of the beast, she thought. In the suites above me people live in unbelievable luxury and down here is the world – the only world I'll probably ever know. 'But who the hell cares?' she said out loud. 'You're young and you're beautiful, Marisa. Just don't ever forget that.'

She moved into the room-service kitchen, the Pointer Sisters blasting out 'Yes I Can' on somebody's radio, mixed with the cacophony of room service waiters loading breakfast carts. Marisa admired the organized mayhem. Somehow the work got done, and done right.

A young waiter waved to her, showing a toothy grin. 'Yo – Marisa.'

' 'Sup, Steve?'

The cook, Miss Victor, was barking out orders like a Marine sergeant. 'People, pay attention to your set ups. No mistakes. Let's make it a peaceful morning.'

From the kitchen Marisa entered the seamstress shop, a cubbyhole in the basement that seemed to have been carved out of rock and was filled with neat piles of mending. Lily Kim, a slim pretty Korean in her mid-twenties, wearing cropped hair and heavy, hip eye shadow, was bent over a sewing machine.

' 'Sup, Lily.'

Without looking up, she said, 'They're behind the door.'

Marisa took down a pair of altered jeans on a hangar. 'Thanks, Lily. What do I owe you?'

The young woman stopped the machine and glanced at

Marisa with a sly smile. 'I hear the Beresford has some nice new guest slippers.'

Marisa nodded. 'You got it.'

'And I'm running low on the Kiehl's shampoo.'

'No problem. Anything else?'

Lily shrugged. 'Whatever you can pry loose. I'm always in the market for stuff.'

'Bring your handbag to lunch. Empty.'

'My very big handbag.'

'Bigger the better,' Marisa said, laughing. 'Later.'

'Later, girl.'

Marisa ducked out and continued on to the uniform area. A TV droned in the background and she could hear Diane Sawyer interviewing someone. She spotted Clarice LaPointe, a buxom black woman with a quick wit. ' 'Sup, Clarice?'

'Same old.'

Marisa gestured toward the TV. 'Must be something to have breakfast in bed and watch the morning shows. Have to try it sometime.'

'Sure. Dream on.'

They stood in line with the other maids who were picking up their uniforms. Nearby, Paula Burns, head of housekeeping, was addressing three, newly hired maids.

'Remember, girls, a Beresford maid is expedient. A Beresford maid is thorough.'

Clarice gagged and rolled her eyes. 'A Beresford maid steals what isn't nailed down,' she whispered to Marisa.

'A Beresford maid serves with a smile,' Paula Burns continued. 'And the most important quality for you to remember as you begin your careers as Beresford maids is to aspire to be' – she paused here for dramatic effect – 'invisible.' A few of the others, Clarice most dramatically, mouthed the word along with her.

Paula Burns pointed to a picture hanging on the wall of the employee of the month. She wore a bright smile and a wide-eyed expression, which virtually shouted: 'I am sweet and innocent.' The caption beneath it read: *Aspire to serve, aspire to be invisible.*

Clarice leaned close to Marisa and whispered, 'Maybe one day we'll just disappear altogether.'

Marisa stifled a laugh as she picked up her uniform and carried it to the locker room. Her closest friend at the Beresford, Stephanie Kehoe, was seated at the locker next to hers already changing. Stephanie, dark haired and sharp featured, was a few years older than Marisa; she spoke with a Canarsie accent, was forever plagued with man trouble, and possessed a heart of gold under her rough exterior. She was Ty's favorite of all his mother's friends. He called her 'auntie.'

' 'Sup, girl,' Marisa said as she quickly began to undress.

'You know what I just heard? Christina's history after the first.'

'Christina kitchen or Christina assistant manager?'

'Assistant manager,' Stephanie replied. 'And you know what that means.'

'Change.'

'Yeah – change and opportunity.'

'Means someone else is gonna be bustin' my ass on the second floor, is what it means.'

Clarice plumped down with her uniform and Stephanie said, 'How they hangin', babe?'

When Clarice laughed her entire body joined in and jiggled. 'Bigger'n yours, girl. That's how they be hangin'.'

Barbara Norris, a slender woman with tired lines in her face and highlighted blond hair, gave Stephanie a noogie on her arm.

'Hey, Barb, you heard? Christina's history.'

'Good riddance. A bitch on wheels.'

'We'll be getting a new assistant manager.'

'Anything's gonna be an improvement over her high and mighty ass.'

'We still on for happy hour?'

'You bet, Steph. Ten hours and counting.'

Stephanie turned back to Marisa who was tying her white shoes.

'So?'

'So?' Marisa looked up. 'What's this "so" stuff, Steph? What are you saying to me?'

Stephanie stepped in front of Marisa and slammed her locker shut.

'Don't be dense. What do I have to do, beat some sense into you? Don't you get it?'

'Get *what*?'

'There is an opening here. There is an opportunity, is what I'm sayin'. It could be you, Maris.'

Marisa did not reply. She reopened her locker and stuffed her clothes inside.

'Don't you see?' Stephanie went on. 'Nobody knows how this place runs better than you do. You're smart, you work hard, the staff likes you and so do the guests. You're the perfect candidate.'

'Jesus, Steph, why don't you give me a break? They're not going to hire a maid as manager. No way.'

'Assistant manager. Why not? It's a new day.'

'Says who?'

'Says I. Anything's possible. Take me for instance. Starting last night I cleansed my system of all toxic poisons.'

'You stopped smoking? I *know* you didn't give up booze, you lush.'

'I stopped Bobby.'

Marisa slammed her locker door shut and walked over to the bank of mirrors. The Beresford was liberal with mirrors; they wanted to encourage their maids to look presentable.

'Um hmmm,' Marisa said. 'Sure. I've heard that one before.'

'You think I'm kidding?'

'Now why would I think a thing like that?'

'Spare me the sarcasm.'

'Today's Friday, right?'

'So?'

'So you only break up with Bobby on the second Tuesday of every month. It's a thing with you.'

'Not necessarily, Miss Smart Mouth.'

'And certainly never on a weekend.'

'That's not true. Barb and I are going drinking tonight.'

'Would you stop already? It's embarrassing, Steph. I mean it's sad. You break up with the guy, the next day you're back. And how long has that been going on. Eleven years? Twelve?'

They talked to each other's reflection as they applied fresh makeup.

'Thirteen, next month,' Stephanie said with a touch of sadness. 'Which is my exact point. So I say to him, "You know, Bobby, come October our relationship hits adolescence." '

'Cute.'

'Yeah, and he goes, "OK – so?" Like he just doesn't get it. And I go, "So thirteen years you been getting the milk for free. It's time to buy the cow already." '

'You said that? Jesus, Steph, comparing yourself to a *cow*?'

'I thought it made the point.'

'So what did he say?'

'He just laughed like it was all a big joke. Haw-haw-haw. Big hollow laughter. Frankly, though, I think the dumb lug is scared out of his mind.'

'He's a man. At least I agree with the dumb part.'

Stephanie sighed and shook her head. 'I don't know, Maris – something just snapped in me. Badda bing, like that. It was like, Who needs it, what's the point? So I just turned around and walked real slow, like, so he could remember my ass, saying, " 'Bye, 'bye." ' She demonstrated for her friend by snapping her fingers down her rear end like castanets.

'Get out of here! You did that?'

'I did, and it gets better. Me and my gorgeous ass strolled across the street to Nick's. You know Nick's.'

'Yeah. Ladder company goes there off shift, right?'

'It's like a candy store for big girls – you know what I'm sayin'?'

'This better be true. I'm going to kill you, girl, if this is some jive job.'

'Swear to God, hope to die. I sit down, order my Jack and ginger and say to this hunky mustache next to me, I say "You're one of New York's bravest. I got thirteen years of being faithful to get out of my system. You brave enough to be the first one in?" '

'Damn, *damn*,' Marisa cried. She gave her friend a high-five. 'Way to go, girl. Now just how beautiful is that?'

3

The long Beresford day of service and invisibility was about to begin. Marisa, Barbara, Stephanie and Clarice joined thirty other maids, butlers, bell men and valets for the morning staff meeting with John Bextrum, the hotel's manager. The caste difference within the ranks of employees was clear to the discerning eye. The maids stayed strictly to themselves, as did the butlers, bell men and valets. 'It's sort of like the old plantation South,' Clarice once explained for her friends' amusement. 'You had the slaves workin' in the mansion – you know, that would be like the butlers. Especially Lionel. Then you had the field slaves. That's us. The real workers.'

Lionel Bloch, elegant, grim-visaged and bald, in his fifties, entered the room and nodded to the assembled group. Impeccably dressed in a dark blue pinstripe suit, white shirt and a blue silk tie, Lionel was Beresford's chief of butlers and as close to management as you could be without actually being management.

Paula Burns, clipboard in hand, raised her voice to be heard over the din. 'Good morning, people,' she began, flashing a practiced smile on and quickly off again. 'Quiet, please. Mr Bextrum has an announcement to make. Mr Bextrum?'

John Bextrum, in his mid-thirties, carried himself with the gravity of a much older man. His manner was polished, dry and vaguely menacing. Beady eyes and a small weak mouth kept him from handsomeness. Clarice liked to say that he confused himself with God. 'And I know a secret about the man,' she once confided to Marisa and Stephanie over cocktails. 'John likes to act so high and mighty and hoity-toity, doesn't he? Like a Princeton boy or somethin'. Well, Marie Tomlin – in payroll? – she told he never even went to college. He's just all made up.'

Bextrum's eyes scanned the group for a moment, his expression flat. 'As I believe you're all aware, Christina Howard is leaving us. Her departure creates a vacancy we'd like to fill within house personnel.' He cleared his throat. 'That is the Beresford way.'

Stephanie leaned close to Marisa and said, 'Told you. . . .'

Bextrum gestured toward the knot of butlers, bell men and valets. 'Perhaps one of you – Joe, Rob, Tom, any one of you – perhaps you would consider management. There's a splendid opportunity here.'

Marisa turned to Stephanie, smirking, and whispered, 'Told *you*. Look which direction the man is looking. You can forget it.'

'There is nothing more rewarding,' Bextrum continued weightily, 'than growing your own, so to speak. Applications are on the table against the wall.'

Stephanie raised her hand, waving it wildly, trying to get Paula Burns' attention.

'Excuse me – Mr Bextrum. Sir?'

'What is it, Stephanie?' Burns said, a curt edge to her voice.

'Can a maid apply?'

Clarice whispered, 'What is she, nuts?'

Paula Burns turned to Bextrum with a slight shrug as though to say, You field this one; this is what you're paid for.

He rubbed his chin as he stared at Stephanie. 'Can a . . . ahh . . . well.' He nodded. 'A good question, Ms Kehoe. Technically, of course, if an employee's been here for three consecutive years, he or . . . *she* . . . is qualified to apply.' He forced a grin. 'So why not, I suppose. Anything's possible, and you are certainly within your rights. Does that answer your question?'

'Yes sir,' Stephanie answered brightly. She turned to Marisa and nudged her. 'He says anything's possible. Didn't I tell you?'

'Quiet,' Marisa hissed. 'You're attracting attention.'

Paula Burns clapped to bring the room back to order. 'There will be a small staff party in Miss Howard's honor, day after tomorrow from five till seven. We'll hold it in the cafeteria to accommodate shift changes.'

Barbara whispered, 'Otherwise they'd have had it at Le Cirque.'

Stephanie stifled a laugh with her hand. 'It's the Beresford way,' she said, doing a sharp imitation of John Bextrum.

'So – on to business,' Paula Burns said as she examined her clipboard with a near-sighted squint. 'Mr Radcliffe is checking out of seven-oh-nine. Mr Greenwald is checking in. He's back on the wagon, so let's clean out the mini-bar.

'Kanga CFO Mr Fukimoro is checking into eight-fourteen. Stock extra Evian, shampoo the carpets and make certain there are extra slippers for his guests. . . . Oh, yes, and avoid eye contact, please, ladies. We've had complaints in the past.

'Stephanie, Marisa, when we're finished here you'll head on to the Madison Suite. Mr Lassiter's girlfriend is due to depart by noon. Mrs. Lassiter and children are arriving from Chicago, ETA, two-thirty.' The faintest trace of a smile crossed Paula Burns' stern countenance. 'Let's make sure it's an orderly transition.'

'Oh goody,' Clarice said sotto voce. 'More fun and games at the old Beresford.'

Paula squinted at her notes. 'We also have two VIPs checking into suites today. Sotheby's Director, Caroline Lane, in the Park Suite. She's coming over from the Four Seasons. Rather demanding, I'm told. She favors Pratesi bed linens and orchids, San Pellegrino flat. Her favorite scent is lavender.

'And in the York Suite, from Albany, we have Assemblyman Christopher Marshall. The Suite will be doubling as a conference center, so we'll be turning over the liquor and coffee bars every four hours.' Paula Burns paused, took a deep breath and squinted at her clipboard again. 'Mr Marshall favors Anchor Steam beer and almond crusted tuna from Nellie's on Houston. Extremely important point – being a politician he *must have* all the New York and Washington papers, plus the *Journal*. And he's bringing his large dog. We will need proper accoutrements.'

Paula slapped her clipboard against her side, military style. 'That's it, people. Service and invisibility. Let's go!'

The maids quickly set up for their day in the well-stocked shelving area. Precisely and without a wasted movement, they packed linens, silverware, coffee, napkins, glasses, copies of the *Times*, *USA* and the *Wall Street Journal*. Marisa and

Stephanie, pushing their carts crammed with supplies, took the freight elevator to the second floor, to the Madison Suite embossed in gold lettering. They quietly entered. Mr Lassiter's girlfriend had done a thorough job of trashing the place – lamps were turned over, breakfast was smeared all over the floor, clothes were scattered everywhere, cigarettes were burning in two ashtrays. And a very unhappy, very elegantly dressed young woman turned to Marisa and Stephanie with a teary, don't-mess-with-me look. She rose unsteadily and hurled a crystal lamp against the wall, just missing the window. She then marched into the bathroom and slammed the door.

'Whew,' Marisa said, rolling her eyes.

'The love birds musta had a real peachy night,' Stephanie said. 'Jesus, what a mess. Mr L. is gonna have some bill.'

'I'm sure he deserves it,' Marisa said. 'We better get this show on the road.' She plugged in the radio they had brought with them and hit the CD button. The music had a strong R&B beat, and Marisa and Stephanie danced as they cleaned, both together and separately. In two hours the Suite was as good as new.

The Adams Suite was also a mess, and Marisa worked through lunch into the early afternoon. The Park Suite was a different story altogether. The outgoing guest had barely left a trace of habitation; within an hour Marisa, working alone now, had it ready for the next occupant, the Sotheby's Director, Caroline Lane. A demanding lady, huh? Marisa thought, as she put the finishing touches on the room. They all are. She fanned a selection of glossy magazines on the coffee table. What is it with these rich people anyway? Never satisfied, nothing ever good enough, or quite up to their standards. It seems like the more they get the more they crave. There's no end to it. I wonder if I'd be like that if I was rich.

She placed a flowering orchid on the writing desk, placing it just so as she'd been taught: not centered but slightly, artfully off to one side. 'It adds a touch of class,' Paula Burns had told her when she started at the Beresford. You never had to tell Marisa anything twice; she listened closely and never forgot.

Before finishing in the Park Suite, Marisa placed an envelope addressed to 'Ms Caroline Lane' on the table and set a sprig of fresh lavender on the bolster pillow. As she took a last look around, nodding in approval, Paula Burns burst into the room. She moved to the bed and picked up the lavender sprig.

'What a nice touch,' she exclaimed. 'You're very creative, Marisa.'

'Thank you, ma'am.'

'I put you right at the top of my list. You're always learning and improving.'

'I appreciate that.'

'Go find Lionel and have him sign off on the Suite.'

'Right away.'

Lionel was in the York Suite where he was inspecting Stephanie and Barbara's work before signing off on it in the small notebook he carried everywhere. He double-checked the stock in the refrigerator as a bell man put several bags from Nellie's inside. Lionel nervously repositioned the newspapers on the table as another bell man brought in a large dog bed and started toward the bathroom with it.

'No, no, Damon,' Lionel said. 'I'm sure the master will want his dog sleeping beside his bed. Put it there.'

When Marisa entered the York Suite Lionel was inspecting the selection of men's toiletries in the bathroom. 'Lime,' he muttered. 'Did Paula say lime or bay rum?' He shook his head, annoyed at himself. He just couldn't remember what she'd told him; it seemed that there were so many details he couldn't remember these days. To be on the safe side, he would have to start write everything down.

As Marisa watched him at the open door to the bathroom his hands began to tremble and the bottle of men's cologne slipped from his grasp and crashed to the marble floor. Instinctively he reached down for it and a shard of glass cut his finger. He cupped his bloody hand in the other and stared at it. 'Damn!' he said.

He turned to see Marisa standing at the bathroom entrance and his eyes slid away from her, his jaw working with tension. She realized that she had just witnessed something that she wasn't supposed to see.

'I need you to sign off on the Park, sir,' she said quickly.

He started to answer when his beeper went off. He reached for it with his good hand.

'Oh God, he's checking in. He's early.'

Marisa advanced a step and said, 'Here, let me help you.'

'I've got it, Miss Ventura. I'm fine. Really.'

'You have a pretty deep cut,' she said. She wet a washcloth and pressed it to his hand, politely but firmly. 'I'll finish up in here, sir.' She reached for a bottle of aspirin, shook out two tablets and handed them to Lionel with a glass of water. 'You better take these.'

'Thank you,' he said.

After swallowing the pills he bent down and began picking up the slivers of glass.

'No,' she said, 'I can clean this up quick. You really need to check that hand.'

For a moment he looked uncertain, then he said, 'Once the Assemblyman is settled in, I'll take care of it.'

Duty first, she thought. She was very fond of Lionel, a stern butler who had devoted his life to service. She was sure that he was a dying breed.

They both stiffened as they heard the door to the York Suite open. The first sound they heard was the deep barking of a dog.

4

At the very moment that Lionel cut himself, Christopher Marshall was hopping out of his town car followed by Jerry Seigal and a female assistant. Bell men gathered up the luggage as Marshall and Seigal hurried to the Beresford entrance. Seigal was outlining the day's plans, while Marshall, oblivious both to Seigal's steady stream of chatter and the celebrity gawkers pushing close to them, turned around looking for his dog Rufus. The dog bounded out of the trailing van that had just drawn up to the curb and an assistant quickly grabbed his leash.

When they entered the York Suite, Lionel was there to greet them, hands clasped behind his back, the washcloth wrapped like a tourniquet around his injured hand. Seigal brushed by him without acknowledgement, reading aloud from a newspaper. Chris Marshall and the assistant trailed after the feisty chief of staff, and the bell men, wheeling in a trolley laden with luggage, brought up the rear.

Marshall removed Rufus' leash and collar as Seigal continued to read. 'Quote . . . "sentimental favorite, Chris Marshall" . . . na na na na na na . . . "son of the late Senator Grant

Marshall" . . . na na na na na . . . "who's expected to run for his father's seat in next year's senatorial election" . . . unquote.' Seigal grinned up at Marshall. 'I think it's totally respectful.'

Marshall grabbed the paper from him. 'Let me see that.'

'Hey, I wasn't finished.'

'I can see that, Jerry. You were far from finished. Too busy editing the news.' He began to read out loud: ' "Sentimental favorite, and playboy politico Assemblyman Chris Marshall. . . ." ' He looked up from the paper and his expression wasn't happy. 'Guess you missed a few words there, didn't you?'

'So what? Calling you a playboy, that's a compliment. It sure didn't hurt JFK, it didn't hurt Clinton.'

'Jesus, Jerry, the man was impeached.'

'So? He never lost his popularity.'

Marshall returned to the paper. ' ". . . .Chris Marshall who called off his engagement last month to über-babe Daniella Von Graas, arrived in town solo. . . ." ' He tossed the paper on the floor and wagged a finger under Seigal's chin. 'Respectful, huh? That's your idea of respectful?'

Seigal shrugged. 'So you're a public figure. It's news, babe. You sneeze, it's news. Get used to it.'

'We were never engaged!' Marshall raised his voice in a rare loss of control. 'Jesus, man, whose side are you on anyway?'

'Yours, and that's why I'm telling you how much you need me. You need to be pushed. You're almost too much of a gentleman for this profession, Chris. You and Bill Bradley – the last of a dying breed.'

'Al*most* too much of a gentleman,' Marshall said ruefully. 'But clearly not quite.'

He turned away, got on his hands and knees and began

playing with Rufus, who wagged his tail and slobbered with happiness.

'Chris,' Seigal said, standing over him, 'if I can interrupt your important conference for a moment. Look at me, please.'

'I don't want to look at you. Can't you see I'm busy?'

'We're going to Maddox's thing Monday night. I'm serious.'

Marshall shook his head as he rubbed Rufus behind his ears. 'No, Jerry, we aren't.'

He got up and headed for the bathroom.

'If only your old man were here,' Seigal said. 'He'd support me on this.'

'Are you kidding? My father had no use for that man.'

'No, wrong,' Seigal said to Marshall's retreating back. 'Your father knew how to use that man.'

Marshall, about to enter the bathroom, cast his chief of staff a puzzled look. 'Where are you going, Jerry?'

'That depends. Where are you going?'

'Bathroom, OK? Alone.' He walked in and started to close the door when Seigal said, 'Call me if you need anything.'

Marshall opened the door again and looked around it, his eyebrow raised. 'What?'

'Hey, just joking. A little levity, babe. Got to keep things loose.'

Marshall shook his head and again disappeared into the bathroom.

Seigal whirled around and glared at Lionel and the bell man. 'What's with the big ears, huh? Haven't you guys got something to do?'

'Ease up, Jerry,' Marshall yelled out. 'You're too hyper.' He stood at the commode and unzipped his fly.

Marisa, still on her hands and knees looking for the last glints of glass, loudly cleared her throat and rose to her feet. She turned away from him, toward the bathtub.

'Oh, my goodness, I'm sorry,' Marshall said, surreptitiously zipping up his fly. 'I didn't know anyone was in here.'

'I'm sorry,' Marisa said. 'I was just – there was some glass on the floor. I'm finished.'

Keeping her head down, she rushed from the room. She hurried to the pantry where Lionel was trying unsuccessfully to remove a shard of glass from his finger. His hand was trembling.

'Let me help you, sir.'

He glanced at her and allowed himself the ghost of a smile. 'You seem to be doing little else than helping me today.'

She took down a first aid kit from a shelf of medical supplies and unscrewed a tube of antiseptic cream and a needle. She lit a match, heated the needle and quickly removed the sliver; she then applied the cream and a bandage.

'You're very efficient, Miss Ventura.'

'I have a ten-year-old boy. I'm used to this.'

Lionel sighed and looked away. 'I'm afraid I'm rather clumsy.'

'It happens to all of us.'

'Thank you for your help.' He forced his shoulders back as he said, 'I need to do some fast catch-up now. I'm behind on my inspections.'

Marisa noticed a garment bag hanging on a coat rack against the wall. It carried the Dolce and Gabbana logo.

'Where do these go?' she said.

'Caroline Lane,' Lionel answered. 'In the Park Suite. She

just checked in with a réquest for immediate unpack and press. I'd better take it to her. She's rather, ah, I sense a certain amount of temperament.'

'Blood and Dolce,' Marisa said. 'Um hm.'

Lionel smiled slightly and nodded.

'I'm going by the Park Suite anyway,' Marisa said, grabbing the bag. 'I can take it to her.'

On the twenty-second floor she stood at the door, took a deep breath and knocked softly. 'Housekeeping,' she said. When there was no response she used her passkey to enter. She stopped by the coffee table, clicked on music with the remote, lowering the volume to barely above a whisper, and continued into the bedroom. As she hung the garment bag in the closet she heard the corridor door open. She turned to see a bell man come in pushing half a dozen pieces of T. Anthony luggage on a trolley. Following behind, chatting animatedly into a cell phone, was a slender, blond, fashionably dressed woman in her early thirties. Marisa took her in in an instant. She knew the type; the Beresford had been created for women like her: well-born, well bred, imperious and entitled. Marisa was aware that Caroline Lane made frequent appearances in the gossip columns. She was a staple item in the *New York Post*'s Page Six, where an unnamed source had once said of her: 'Caroline is neither as shallow and deluded as her detractors hope she is, nor as captivating and irresistible as she thinks she is.'

Marisa picked up those juicy bits of gossip from Stephanie, who read the tabloids religiously and could be depended on to tell you who was sleeping with whom and who was spending time in the Betty Ford Clinic and who had recently sold his waterfront property in the Hamptons for a ten-million-dollar loss.

'What the hell is it with him anyway?' Caroline said into the phone as she dropped a copy of *The Observer* over the carefully arranged fan of magazines. 'I mean he's made it crystal clear – *more* than crystal clear, you know. A clinging vine, not independent enough. You think I'm going to beg him to come with me on a business trip? Not in this lifetime. . . .'

She absently tossed her scarf over the orchid as she paced the room.

'Well, honestly, the whole entire thing is up and down. One day we're looking at rings, the next day we're breaking up. It's so absolutely *mad*dening. *Any*thing can happen here. We're at crisis time, Rach.'

She punctuated that statement by flinging her coat over the lavender sprigs on the bed, obliterating yet another of Marisa's thoughtful touches. Caroline Lane kicked off her shoes and sprawled out on the bed, and grinning into the phone said in conspiratorial tones, 'So . . . listen to *this*. I had my assistant 'accidentally' forward my calendar for the week to his e-mail. Of course I added a few extra lunch dates and dinner parties with my ex. Eric will be simply furious. Fan*tas*tic, right?'

She giggled. 'You have to be like the CIA with these men. Always plotting. Hold on a sec.'

She held out a five-dollar bill to the bell man without glancing at him, and pointed to Marisa, who was once again straightening the magazines. Covering the mouthpiece, she said, sotto voce, 'All that stuff needs pressing.' She gestured to her bags.

'Yes, ma'am.' Marisa started unpacking, and as she held items up, Caroline Lane made an 'ironing' gesture with her free hand.

40

Maybe she thinks I don't understand English. Maybe she thinks I just sailed in on a raft and picked up my green card. Bitch.

Caroline returned to her conversation, saying, 'Because here's the point, the point I'm getting at, Rach, I mean here's what I've learned. Men do not marry you unless they think someone else wants you. They are stupid – let's face it – and have to be manipulated. Let's not forget, Eric trades commodities for a living. A little competition right now might increase my market value.' She listened impatiently, then checked her watch. 'Shoot, I'm running really late. Catch you later.'

She snapped the phone shut as Marisa gathered up the pressing and started to leave.

'Wait just a sec?'

She languorously rose from the bed and walked to the closet and quickly examined the three outfits from Dolce and Gabbana. She removed one dress and held it to the light.

'Hmmm. I can't tell without the stockings. Would you do me a big favor?' She continued staring at the dress, not yet making eye contact with Marisa. She then surveyed the room, grabbed a small pillow from the chair and put her finger on a leaf in the pattern.

I'm invisible, Marisa thought. I'm something these people talk at, especially the women. Paula Burns doesn't have to push the idea. These people never see us as human beings anyway.

'Ma'am?'

Caroline Lane finally glanced at her, bestowing on her a sweet smile. 'I know this isn't your job and I'd never ask otherwise, but I'm incredibly tight on time. . . .'

'It's OK,' Marisa said, returning her smile.

'Oh, you're a doll. Could you run and get me three pairs of panty hose – one the exact shade of the leaf in this pattern' – she thrust the pillow at Marisa – 'one a tad darker and one a smidge lighter. The thing is, I'm in a jam.'

'Well, the concierge usually takes care of these things.'

Caroline shook her head impatiently. 'It'll get lost in translation, trust me. Please! You look like someone who knows the difference between taupe and caramel.'

In spite of herself Marisa felt a warm flush. She liked the compliment.

'Here.' Caroline grabbed a handful of bills from her wallet and waved them at Marisa. 'That should cover it, and again, thank you *so much*. You've saved my life.'

Trotting down the corridor with the pillow and an armload of pressing, Marisa passed two elderly, expensively dressed French women who were busy liberating a cart of its toiletries.

'Oohh, look at this cream,' said the plump one in French. 'We didn't have *this* in our room.' She opened the bottle. 'Smells delicious. You should try it, Monique.'

'No, no,' said the petite one. 'It's not for me, Anouk. Too rich.'

'How about this one then?'

'Let me see.'

As they talked they stuffed items into their purses, and when they saw Marisa approaching they stopped immediately and switched to heavily accented English.

'Lovely weather,' Anouk said, with a wary eye on Marisa.

'Do you think it will rain?' Monique said.

Marisa passed them, eyes averted, suppressing a laugh, and raced toward the pantry.

'Who knows? It may,' Anouk said. When Marisa disappeared through the door, she continued in French, saying, 'She's gone. Let's hurry.'

They quickly grabbed more products from the cart.

Stephanie was coming out of the parlor room as Marisa headed in. They nearly bumped into each other.

'Hey, Maris, where's the fire, girl?'

'Ty's speech starts at four,' she said breathlessly. 'Arlene's covering for me. I'm really racing.' She shoved the clothes at her friend. 'Get these pressed for me, OK?'

'Oh sure. In my spare time – and you of all people know I have nothing but.'

Marisa had already left the room, then she reappeared and said, 'Oh, almost forgot. Two old French poodles in the corridor are picking your cart clean.'

'What?' Stephanie peered down the hall and watched the two ladies feverishly stuffing their purses.

'Well, I'll be a son of a bitch,' she exclaimed, turning to Marisa who was already gone.

She ran to the nearest women's store two blocks from the Beresford on Lexington Avenue and searched for someone to help her. She sensed that people were staring at her, and she felt uncomfortable in her maid's uniform. She approached the counter; the sales clerk was preoccupied on the telephone. Marisa tried to speak to her and got no response. She shrugged and headed for the backroom.

The clerk, eyeing her, said into the phone, 'Hold one second.' To Marisa she said in much sharper tones, 'Miss . . . excuse me, where are you going?'

'In back to see if Carrie is—'

The clerk cut her off. 'She's off today. Would you please move away. . . . Just move away from there. . . . Please.' She returned to her phone conversation as Marisa waited. 'Hi. Sorry. No, nothing. No one. You go first. C'mon, *tell* me. No, you go. No – *you*.' She giggled, oblivious to the line that was forming behind Marisa. 'Now Chris, you can't keep *that* from me. . . .'

'Excuse me?' Marisa said.

The clerk howled with laughter into the phone. 'Are you *serious*? Get out! Get out of here!'

'I'm sorry,' Marisa said, 'but I'm in a hurry.'

The clerk tried to stare down Marisa, her mouth tightening, and extended her hand, palm out, as though she was halting traffic. She then turned her back and continued talking. 'So go on. Then what happened? No he didn't. *No he didn't.* You're making that up. He *did*?' She screeched laughter again. 'Ahhhh. I *love* it.'

Marisa leaned across the counter. 'Can I ask you if—'

Again the clerk cut her off. 'You'll have to wait,' she hissed. She returned to the phone. 'What? Oh, a maid. I don't know.' She spoke just loud enough for Marisa to hear. She added, 'They're letting anyone in here now, you know what I'm saying? Got to watch 'em like hawks. So? Go on. What did he do then?'

Marisa leaned as close as she could to the clerk and said in her ear, 'Yo?'

The clerk suddenly found herself nose to nose with Marisa, who flicked her nametag with one finger. 'Leezette,' she said.

'You just stay on your side of the counter. You have no right to—'

'Oops.' Marisa took the telephone from the startled clerk.

'What're you doing?'

Marisa hung up the phone. 'Being that we're sisters in the service business and all, Leezette, and being that I'm in kind of a rush, I'd say you start making sales to your low end customers, which is, after all, the reason you're here.'

'You tell her, miss,' said one of the ladies waiting in line. 'This is just ridiculous.'

Marisa waved a hand. 'See the line forming behind me, Leezette? We all want to be waited on, and your job is to wait on us – unless we're not good enough for you to wait on.' She turned to the women behind her. 'What do you say, ladies? Am I right or am I right?'

Their enthusiastic response caused the sales clerk to flinch. 'How can I help you?' she said quietly and with grudging respect.

'Now that's more like it,' Marisa said. She smiled. She felt that she had finally won a round in what was promising to be a very stressed-out day.

5

Veronica Ventura, Marisa's mother, was waiting for her at the Beresford service entrance. In her early fifties and wearing the years well, she was dressed in a conservative gray suit and sensible black walking shoes. She was proud of her daughter – her only child – but their relationship was prickly. She had never quite accepted that her darling Marisa was no longer a child who needed to be protected and lectured to but was a grown woman with a responsible job and a ten-year-old son – 'my boy genius,' Veronica often referred to him with a mixture of fondness and surprise. Mother and daughter sometimes clashed over what Marisa saw as a basic difference in values. Whenever she expressed a desire to improve herself, to rise above her present position, her mother would accuse her of flightiness or dangerous dreaming. 'You're not being realistic,' Veronica would tell her. 'You're lucky you got a good job. It pays the bills. Hang on to it, Marisa. Nothing this good may come along again.'

'I'm just a maid, Ma. It's not exactly a dream position, and I think I'm capable of doing better.' As deeply as the two women loved and respected each other, this argument was old, ongoing and very real.

A few minutes after Mrs. Ventura arrived, Marisa rushed in with the department store bag and spotted Keef sharing a cigarette break with some of the staff.

'Hey, Ma,' Marisa said, blowing her a kiss. 'Be right with you. Keef, do me a favor, will ya? These go to the goddess in the Park Suite. OK? I owe you one.'

Keef nodded. 'I can handle that. No problem.'

'Thanks. You're my God.' She picked up her bags. 'You ready, Ma? I don't have time to change.'

'Sure you do. We'll be a little late.'

'No,' Marisa said firmly. 'Ty will freak out.' She nudged her mother playfully. 'Don't I look presentable enough for you?'

Veronica gave her a quick inspection, from her hair to her shoes. 'You look OK.'

'Just OK?'

'You look fine.'

'Well, come on then.' She tugged at her mother's arm. 'Let's motor, girl.'

'Don't call me girl. I'm your mother.'

At the middle school an overhead banner read: PRESIDENTIAL PRESENTATION: OUR FOUNDING FATHERS. The children crowded around stage left peeking out of the curtains, waving to friends and family in the audience. Ty stood with Tiana and he looked too adult and solemn for a ten-year-old as though he was carrying the weight of the world on his slender shoulders.

Tiana started hopping up and down in excitement. 'There's my dad – and there comes my brother and my Aunt Pat.' She half stepped around the curtain, waving and calling out, 'Hi Daddy— Hi!'

She turned to Ty, who was searching the crowd for his family. 'You see 'em yet?' she asked.

Ty slowly nodded. 'Yeah, they're just coming in – my mom and dad and my grandma.' He waved convincingly – waving to no one.

At that moment Marisa and her mother were walking quickly toward the subway, two blocks away. Marisa kept glancing at her watch: three-thirty. With a break they would be on time. Just then her cell phone rang inside her bag, and without breaking stride she fished it out and opened it.

'Yeah,' she said. 'Marcus? It's hard to hear you. Where are you? You've got half an hour and you can't be late. Ty's gonna have a fit. Hello? *Marcus*? You're breaking up. These cells . . .' Marisa gave the phone a dirty look. 'I can't keep – *what*? Please tell me you're kidding.'

She stopped short, causing her tote bag to fall from her shoulders, the contents spilling onto the pavement.

'I'll get it,' Veronica said. She retrieved a wallet, a comb, gum wrappers, an address book, a nail clipper, a check book, an application form, various receipts and scribbled notes and phone numbers, and two CDs – 'Best of Moody Blues' and 'The Nixon Tapes'. She stuffed everything back into the bag except for the application form.

As they walked down the steps to the subway entrance, Marisa was growing more agitated. She swiped her Metro Card viciously through the slot. 'Don't do this to me, Marcus. Most of all you're hurting Ty, you know.'

'Don't let him get away with it,' Veronica said, her face pinched with anger.

'So what do I tell him this time?' Marisa said into the phone. 'I don't think there's one valid excuse left. You've used them up.'

'You can't give into him, Marisa. Be strong.'

'Shut up, Ma.' Marisa shook her head, glaring at the phone. The subway arrived and they stepped inside.

'I mean, Jesus,' she said into the phone, 'this weekend was the camping trip. Do you have any idea how much he's been counting on this?' She listened, continuing to shake her head. 'No, Marcus, *no*. Save it for somebody who believes you. . . . I got to go.' She closed the phone with an angry snap and shoved it in her bag. Mother and daughter sat side by side in silence. The silence began to trouble Marisa because Veronica was usually so voluble it was hard to slip in a word.

'What?' Marisa said finally, glancing at her.

'I'm not saying anything.'

'Can you not say anything with a little less attitude?'

'If I'd talked to my mother like that she'd have slapped me.'

'Different times, Ma. We got family democracy now.'

She began to fix her hair and her makeup, tapping her foot impatiently, willing the train to go faster.

'So what's his excuse this time?'

'I don't want to talk about it.'

After another short, brooding silence Veronica said, 'So what's this? It fell out of your bag.' She handed Marisa the Beresford application form.

'Oh yeah. . . . Thanks.' She studied her mother. 'I see it didn't find its way back into my bag.'

'Management, huh? Fancy.'

Marisa folded the form and dropped it into her tote bag.

She tried to ready herself for what she knew was coming. 'Don't start up, Ma.'

'Did I tell you I saw Carmen Suza's niece Lupe last Sunday?'

Marisa sighed. 'No, you didn't tell me.'

'You remember Lupe, right? You played together when you were little.'

'So?'

'So she was this big deal at Sanyo. Her own office with a window. And a secretary she didn't even have to share with anybody. But one day she decided to ask for more. Guess what she got.'

'Ma, I told you not to start up with me, especially right now. It's obvious you think Lupe had no right to ask for more.'

'She was fired, Marisa. They let her go. *That's* what she got, see? You see what I mean?'

'I'm not going to fight with you. I'm just not.'

'The thing I'm trying to tell you is, they think you're unhappy in your present position they give it to somebody else who wants it. And the job you want – the one you dream about – well, there's a million people more qualified. Look at me, honey. Look at me.'

Marisa turned to her. 'I hope you know how much I hate this conversation.'

'People who dream end up with kids at nineteen, tied to a loser.'

Marisa stared straight ahead, trying to blot out her mother's words. Part of her feared that her mother might be right.

The speakers were on stage in the auditorium before a packed audience, sitting under the banner OUR FOUNDING FATHERS. Ty listened as a confident Tiana concluded her speech at the podium.

'Abraham Lincoln's policies,' she said in forceful tones, 'were bold and brave, and they were unwelcome with most states outside of the union. Lincoln knew he was in for a fight, but he stood by what he believed. . . .'

Her speech received hearty applause and even a few whistles from boys who admired Tiana for reasons other than her speaking ability. Ty was hardly aware that his hands were clapping as he peered anxiously into the audience for his family. At that moment Marisa and Veronica were racing through the turnstiles and up the stairs, a block and a half from the school. Marisa checked her watch – four minutes to four. Ty was due to give his speech at four. She began pawing wildly through her tote bag. 'Where *are* they? Did I forget Ty's presents?'

'They're there – the CDs? I saw them.'

'Oh yeah,' Marisa said after digging further in her bag. 'Thank God.'

'You're a nervous wreck.'

'Thanks for the observation.'

'Why do you get him those 'Nixon Tapes'? The boy doesn't fit in as it is. You think those help? You need to steer him, Marisa, give him some direction. Maybe you should think about Harry Potter books or a baseball mitt.' She was beginning to puff in an effort to stay up with Marisa. 'Can you slow down a little?'

'We're gonna be late. I can't let him start without me.'

'The thing about Ty, he's a little strange already. We don't want to make it worse—'

'Look, Ma,' Marisa said, whirling on her, 'Ty's a smart kid. He soaks up everything he hears, he reads, he sees. Like a sponge, you know? Never stops learning. He's ten and doing eighth grade work, and *that's* too slow for him. The boy is special. So if he wants 'The Nixon Tapes' or anything else you think is strange, I'm gonna get it for him. And nobody – not you, not Marcus – *nobody's* gonna stand in judgment on him. See, he can tell when you're embarrassed or disappointed or uncomfortable. And I don't want him to dumb it up just so you can feel better about him. *Got that?*'

Veronica stared at her daughter open mouthed, and for once she had no comeback. She trotted to stay up with her daughter.

Just as Ty stepped to the podium, he spotted his mother and grandmother entering the auditorium. They waved to him and took seats in the back row. But where was his father? He felt a sinking sensation in the pit of his stomach as he tried to put the thought out of his mind.

'Richard Milhous Nixon,' he began with a stammer and then stopped. The microphone was set too high for him and he had to stand on tiptoe to talk into it. He heard titters from the audience. The assistant principal rushed up and adjusted the mike for him.

'Richard Milhous Nixon,' he began again, 'was a man of many contradictions. Even though he is remembered in history as the only president to ever resign, his foreign policies and his relationship with China opened the Western door to Eastern. . . .' Ty frowned and stared at his notes. 'I mean the Eastern door . . . to West . . . Western ties.' He leaned lower over the podium as though he were trying to hide himself.

'Born a Quaker. . . .'

A kid in the audience mimicked Ty's delivery – 'Born a Quaker. . . .' The tittering grew louder.

'He . . . he was nevertheless . . . um . . . he was responsible for bombing . . . for the violent bombing of . . . um . . . umm . . . of the . . . umm.'

Ty shook his head, swept up his notes and ran off stage.

'Jesus,' Marisa said. She walked purposefully down the center aisle and took a side door that led back stage. Ty was leaning against a wall, shaking and clutching his notes in a ball, but he was dry-eyed.

She held him in a tight embrace; his body was stiff and unresponsive.

'They were all laughing at me,' he said. 'And then everything just went blank. The whole speech wiped out.'

'It happens, honey.'

'I had a bad feeling about this all day. I never want to do it again.'

They were silent for a moment and could hear the confident delivery of another student, his voice deep, already changed. 'Franklin Delano Roosevelt created many solutions to the nation's economic problems. . . .'

'Bobby Hoffman,' Ty said. 'A ninth grader. He sounds good, but he's dumb. He got suspended last year for lifting research wholesale from the internet.' Ty sighed. 'But the point is, he *sounds* good. He makes an impression and I'm a disaster.' He looked at his mother. 'Never again, OK?'

'This isn't the time to discuss it. It's like you just fell off your bike. You don't feel like getting back on right now.'

'I mean it,' he said, his voice rising.

'We'll talk about it later.' She handed him the CDs. 'Here, I got you these.'

He glanced at them. 'Thank you. Where's dad?'

'There's this construction job in Poughkeepsie. . . .'

He nodded, his face empty of expression.

'They're paying him time and a half. That means a lot to him.'

'He'll be there for the weekend?'

'Yes.'

Ty's face tensed as he fought to hide his emotions. 'That's OK.'

'But he's taking you camping next weekend.'

'Next weekend's not a holiday.'

'So? You'll take a couple days off from school. No big deal. You've earned it.'

Ty tried to smile, but then tensed as a teacher approached them. 'Miss Rhoden,' he whispered. 'My homeroom teacher.'

She nodded to Ty, who was studiously examining his sneakers, and said to Marisa, 'May I speak with you for a moment, Ms Ventura?'

'Sure.' She touched Ty's shoulder. 'I'll be right back, honey.'

Marisa followed the teacher to a table in the back of the room.

'I'm concerned that we're putting too much pressure on Ty,' Miss Rhoden began.

'Pressure? You certainly can't mean academic pressure.'

The teacher smiled. 'Hardly that. Your son is probably the smartest student I've ever had in all my years of teaching. Perhaps in a way he's too smart. He has a grown mind in a boy's body and he has to live each day among children. You're

55

aware, aren't you, that he's poorly socialized?'

'Yes.'

'It isn't easy for him. His brilliance sets him apart. I don't know the answer.'

'I don't either,' Marisa said. 'I can't buy him friends.'

'He's the kind of boy who will do much better as the rest of him grows into his intellect. Right now he's all mind. But soon he'll grow stronger, taller, more self-assured.' The teacher rested a hand lightly on Marisa's shoulder. 'You have every reason to be proud of Ty, Ms Ventura. He's a very, very special child. But because he's special he stands out.'

'I know. All I can do is love him and stand by him.' Marisa felt tears building behind her eyes.

'That's all any of us can do,' Miss Rhoden said.

When Marisa returned to Ty he had his headphones on and was deep into the track 'Question' from the new Moody Blues CD. He was happy now. He was no longer in school. He was a million miles away.

6

On Saturday morning Ty did not want to get out of bed. He grumbled that it was the weekend and he had a right to sleep late. Besides, he had homework to do, a book report to write, and he was planning to listen to his new tapes.

'Sorry, kiddo,' Marisa said, ruffling his hair. 'You're spending the weekend at the Beresford. It'll be a nice change of pace for you, OK? You can't stay home anyway because grandma and Abuela both have plans today and tomorrow.'

'I'm old enough to stay by myself.'

'Get up, young man,' she said, giving him a tug, 'before I yank you out. Ten minutes for a shower, I'll have breakfast for you and we're out of here by eight.'

When they arrived at the Beresford, Marisa passed two sales girls from the Valentino shop in the lobby. They were just opening up.

'' 'Sup, Michelle? Frannie?'

'Hi, Marisa,' they said. Frances pinched Ty's arm. 'Hi, cutie.'

He didn't respond. Marisa took off his headphones. 'Ty – Frannie's speaking to you.'

'What? Oh, 'sup, Frannie?'

Marisa shrugged at the girls. 'He's gonna grow headphones right out of his skull one day.'

In the hotel basement, Marisa peeked into the seamstress shop. Lily was already bent over the sewing machine.

'Lily,' Marisa said in a playful, singsong voice. 'We'reee heeereee.'

The Korean girl looked up, smiling. 'You gonna keep me company this morning, Ty? I sure hope so. It gets kinda lonely in here. It's all sewing, stitching, cutting. I could use a little conversation.'

Marisa unpacked his backpack. 'He's got plenty to keep him occupied, right Ty? Puzzles, books, CDs – lots of stuff. He won't be any bother.' She hung up his jacket.

'Ty's never any bother.'

Marisa said, 'C'mere, Ty. You've got something on your face.'

Ty backed away, looking embarrassed. 'I'm not in the mood, Ma.'

Marisa nodded. 'Oooooh-kay. The boy isn't in the mood. I'll be on twenty-two if you need me, Lily. See you at lunch, Ty. Be good.'

He picked up his CD player.

'Hey. . . .'

He looked up.

'You all right?'

'Yeah. I'm cool.'

'I'm really sorry about everything.'

'It's not your fault.'

'Your dad's sorry, too,' she said.

'No he isn't.'

'He really is, Ty. You're wrong. He called last night, I swear he did. You were asleep. He even apologized to me – how about that?'

'He called?'

'Yeah. So give him a break, OK?'

He smiled and did not object when she gave him a hug.

'I wrote a really good speech,' he said, 'even if I messed it up.'

'I know you did. A terrific speech.'

'I love you, Ma.'

'Love you too.'

Lily listened, her eyes glued to the sewing machine, smiling to herself.

Marisa joined the other maids in the supply area where they stocked their carts, chattering away like so many magpies. Stephanie said to Marisa, 'Why so glum? You look like your best friend died, and I know that isn't true seeing your best friend is standing beside you.'

'I'm OK.'

'How did Ty's speech go?'

'It didn't.' Marisa told her the story as she loaded her cart.

'That Marcus. What a total prick.'

'You need to get out and around, girl,' Clarice added.

'Yeah,' Stephanie said. 'You're too uptight. Ty's gonna be fine. You're the one I worry about.'

'I'm *fine*.'

'I could take you to Nick's Friday night.'

Marisa, followed by Stephanie and Clarice, wheeled her

cart down the hall. 'Not interested,' she said as she pressed the elevator button.

'We need fun in our lives,' Stephanie persisted. 'Be spontaneous. Kick up our skirts.'

Marisa looked at her, deadpan. 'Isn't the expression "kick up our heels?" '

'Skirts, heels, whatever. The point is to get out of the rut you're in.'

'I'm with you there, sister,' Clarice said.

Marisa rolled her eyes. 'Neither of you have children. You don't understand responsibilities.'

'All I know is, you only live once,' Stephanie said. 'And you ain't livin', doll. So let's say Nick's next Friday.'

'No.'

'You don't know what you're missing.'

'Maybe I don't. And then maybe I don't care.'

'What are you doing for lunch?'

'Ty's with Lily. I told him I'd pick him up and we'd grab a sandwich.'

'I've got a better plan. I thought maybe we'd have a bite with a few of the guys in shipping. A hot lunch, you know what I'm saying?'

'Sorry, Steph, I can't. I'm not going to saddle Lily with Ty all day.'

'That's just an excuse. You just don't want to meet anybody. What's wrong with you anyway? Why does some man you meet have to be forever? You're old enough to know there's nothing wrong with a good time, no strings attached.'

'There's a difference, Steph, between "forever" and "sorry, I didn't catch your name." Besides, I promised Ty and he has a problem with people who don't keep promises.'

Stephanie nodded, conceding the point. 'Yeah, I know what you mean. He's really a terrific kid.'

'That he is. The best.'

As they pushed their carts down the corridor, Caroline Lane emerged from the Park Suite and stopped directly in front of Marisa, blocking her way.

'Excuse me, aren't you the maid I had yesterday?'

'Yes Ma'am.'

'Excellent. I hope you don't mind, but I need another favor. I'm so late for lunch, otherwise I'd do it myself. You were such a doll yesterday.'

'Thank you.'

'Would you mind running downstairs to the boutique in the lobby and return the outfits in the closet?'

After the briefest of hesitations, Marisa nodded.

'Thank you, thank you, *thank* you. You're just an absolute life saver.'

Caroline Lane turned on her heel and headed for the elevator.

'Who's she?'

'Goddess in the Park Suite. You know, Steph, you two actually have a lot in common.'

'We do? Then why am I the one wearing the uniform?'

'Cute,' Marisa said. They stopped in front of the Park Suite and Marisa reached for her passkey. 'But what I meant was, she's been dating her boyfriend for a while and he hasn't popped—'

'Her cherry?' Stephanie interrupted. 'Because then we'd be twins. I can't even remember when I still had that.'

Marisa shook her head and rolled her eyes.

'What? What are you lookin' at, Miss Purity?'

'Eweee! You're just so nasty, Steph. What you have in common is, he hasn't popped the question.'

'I'm afraid that sounds too familiar.'

'You coming in?' She unlocked the door and went inside.

'Right behind your behind,' Stephanie said.

Marisa began on the bed as her friend walked around checking out Caroline's things, picking them up, putting them back, all the time muttering to herself.

'Here's the difference between me and the Goddess. From what you told me, she's playing games to trick him into wanting her.'

Marisa looked up from a hospital corner she had just made with the bottom sheet. 'And what are you doing?'

'Working hard for the money. Speaking of which, you turn in the application? For management?'

'It's in my locker. I got to finish filling it out.'

'Bet you haven't even started.'

'Think what you want.'

Marisa noticed Stephanie inspecting Caroline Lane's closet, item by item. She unzipped the Dolce garment bags.

'Hey Steph, what are you doing? That's off limits.'

'Dolce. Hmm, nice.'

'Get out of there. You want to get me in trouble?'

'Just a little peek. What's the harm in that?' She took out a matching outfit: a white cashmere, three-quarter length coat, pants and turtle-neck. She caressed them gently and pranced up and down the room like a model doing her swivel parade along a walkway. 'Hellooo,' she breathed. 'Now ladies, what we have here. . . .'

Marisa came up behind her, nervously zipping up the bag. 'Stop it, girl, that's enough. You're scaring me.'

'Feel this material, Maris. Smooth as butter.'

Marisa glanced at the price tag. 'Jeee*sus*. Five thousand dollars!'

'I know – for one white outfit. And it's very impractical. I mean how do you keep it clean for more than one minute. . . .' She shrugged.

'Scotch Guard.'

'But five thousand dollars! These women are insane.'

'That's just the way they are. Money has a whole different meaning for them.'

Stephanie held the outfit up to Marisa and cocked her head back, eyes squinting appraisingly.

'What are you doing now, crazy woman?'

'This is a six. You're a six.'

'So?'

'And the shoes, too – size nine. Perfect.'

'I'm a seven and a half.'

'Which means you're an eight, at least an eight. Put on some gym socks and you're good to go.'

'OK, enough. Put the stuff back.'

'Not until I try this outfit on you. It was made for you, Maris. It honest-to-God was.'

'I can't try on her clothes. Are you nuts?'

'They're not hers. They're going back to Dolce's. She abandoned them. Isn't it wonderful that clothes can't talk? They can't give away our secrets.'

'What are you talking about? You're silly.'

'Come on, Marisa. For God's sake.'

'Come on *what*?'

Stephanie shoved the clothes at her. 'Marisa Ava Maria Ventura, when are you ever going to get to try on a five thousand dollar anything? My guess is, once – and that's now. C'mon – it's time to feel how the other half feels.'

Ty was growing restless. He put down his book, stretched and wandered out of the shop past Lily, who was totally absorbed in her work. The Beresford world through Ty's eyes was very different than through his mother's or his father's. They saw privilege; everything reminded them of the social divide between themselves and the guests who inhabited these impossibly sumptuous suites. For Ty, though, the Beresford was a wonderland of the exotic and unfamiliar – new faces, new clothes, new accents. To Ty, the Beresford world was neither better nor higher on some perceived social scale; it was simply different and therefore exciting. He felt like a lepidopterist – he loved the word – exploring new species of butterflies. He liked to think that he was invisible as he wandered around taking in the sights and sounds.

He got in the first available elevator and, on tiptoe, pressed the button for the twenty-second floor. He pressed that button not because his mother was working there but because it was the penthouse floor – as high as you could go, except for the last elevator, which went to the roof. Ty got a kick out of riding the elevator up and down. When he visited Marisa at the Beresford he would sometimes ride the elevators for hours; it was the best way to observe people – people arriving, departing, dressed to kill or dressed for exercise. Ty, the explorer in a foreign land.

Jerry Seigal paced the floor in the York Suite as he went over the day's schedule with Christopher Marshall. The Assemblyman looked sleepy and bored. Rufus rubbed up against his leg and he absently scratched the dog under his chin.

'There's a league of women voters' lunch starting downstairs in an hour, a little more. We should do a drive-by.'

Marshall shot him a look. 'You mean make a real quick pit stop, huh?' He yawned.

'Ah. I see his highness is in good humor this morning.'

'Why not, Jer? I have you to keep me company. What more could any man want?'

'I choose to ignore that remark.' Seigal studied his notes. 'So . . . the league. We do a fast in and out. Leave 'em laughing.'

Marshall scratched Rufus behind his ears and continued staring at his chief of staff. 'I'd like to ask you a question,' he said. 'And I want an honest answer, OK?'

'Shoot.'

'Do I look as stupid as you think I am?'

'No. . . .' Seigal looked confused. 'Trick question, right? I mean what kind of question is that? You're not stupid. What are you talking about?'

Marshall got to his feet. 'Come on, Rufus. Let's go.'

'Chris, wait,' Seigal said. 'We've got stuff to go over.'

'My dog has more important stuff to do.'

Dog and master left the room, with Seigal in pursuit. Marshall leashed Rufus, strolled into hall and punched the elevator's down button.

'You got a problem with the ladies' lunch? What's with you anyway? This is a shrewd move and it costs us nothing. In and out, like I said.'

'I have a problem trying to upstage Victor Delgado – remember him? The guy running against me for the senate?

The same guy, come to think of it, who's scheduled to speak at the same lunch downstairs.'

'Not till one-thirty,' Seigal said quickly. 'Here's the plan. We slip in, say hello, not a dry seat in the house.' He gave a short bark of laughter. 'The Assemblyman leaves 'em moist.'

Marshall slowly shook his head. 'You're a piece of work, my friend.'

'And believe me, after you work the room with the Marshall charm, Delgado looks like everybody's first husband.'

'*You* listen. Does my mouth move when I talk? Because sometimes I feel I'm in one of those "twilight zones" where I'm screaming and nobody hears me.'

'I hear you, Chris. I just can't listen to you. It's just one roadblock after another – second thoughts, third thoughts, moral objections over nothing at all. You want to be a New York senator? You need to play the game.'

'Oh, I'll play, Jer. But not by your rules.'

'Hey buddy, I didn't write 'em. I'll bet they've been there since George Washington. Do me a favor, please. I know it offends your sense of fairness, but I want to win this election, I want to win it in the worst way. And it's not going to be easy. Think about going to the lunch, and think about Maddox's benefit on Monday.'

Marshall clapped a hand on Seigal's shoulder. 'You just don't give up, do you?'

'That's why you hired me. C'mon, man, what's the big deal? You go to both of them – hello, goodbye, press a little flesh, you leave. Half an hour, max. We're home free.'

As the elevator door opened Marshall said, 'Define "free." '

The two men and the dog entered the elevator. Ty, standing in the back, immediately recognized the tall, fair

Assemblyman. It was strange, he thought, what some people call a coincidence, what others call fate. The man was at his school yesterday, and now here they were riding in the same elevator. He pressed himself against the back of the elevator, trying to make himself invisible.

Seigal said, 'You know, they have these people now that walk your dogs. You give them money, they pick up the doo-doo. Crazy idea, huh?'

'Will you relax, Jerry? You're starting to lose your hair.'

Seigal touched his head, which was almost completely bald. 'Very funny. What a comedian.' Nevertheless, he studied his reflection in the glass pane of the elevator.

Ty had started petting Rufus and the dog rubbed up against his leg, wanting more.

Marshall smiled at the boy. 'What are you listening to?' he said.

Ty removed his headphones. ' "Best of Bread," ' he said.

' "Best of Bread" '? I didn't know they have a "Best of." '

Ty returned his smile. 'They're not my demographic, I know. But I like them a lot.'

Marshall studied the boy closely. 'Not your demographic. How old are you?'

'Ten.'

'What's your name?'

'Ty.'

'Nice to meet you, Ty. I'm Chris.'

'I'm bald,' Seigal put in, 'and no one in particular. Just a guy trying to be heard.'

Ty gave Seigal a startled look and then said to Marshall, 'I know who you are.'

'Oh yeah? What do you know?'

'Well, I know you're a state assemblyman. I know that you're thinking of running for senator. And I know your voting record and your consistent stand on environmental issues.'

Seigal said, 'I hate to interrupt—'

'Then don't,' Marshall said. 'Not now, Jerry.' He turned back to Ty. 'Go on. You were saying. . . .'

'And – I know you miss your dad.'

Marshall was now completely focused on this strange, clearly brilliant young boy. 'Yeah. How do you know that?'

'How could he not?' Seigal said, upset by what he considered a nonessential conversation, and worse, with someone not of voting age.

'Sometimes I miss mine too,' Ty said to Marshall.

'Christ – can I have a minute?' Seigal said.

'Is your father in heaven?' Marshall said, ignoring his chief of staff.

'No,' Ty said. 'Poughkeepsie.'

Marshall smiled at the boy's answer; Seigal did not.

'Are you a Republican?' Ty said.

'Yes.'

'Why are you asking?' Seigal said suspiciously.

'Richard Nixon was a Republican.'

'So?'

'He lied,' Ty said.

Seigal knelt to meet Ty for an eye-to-eye interrogation, which he performed in rapid-fire delivery.

'What does that mean?'

'What I said about Nixon?'

'Yes.'

Ty shrugged. 'Nothing.'

'Who told you to say that?'

'Nobody.'

'What press are you affiliated with?'

'I'm ten.'

'How about your parents – Democrats or Republicans?'

Ty considered his answer for a moment. 'What's the difference these days?'

That answer brought Seigal up short; it was now his turn to take a moment to think out his next question.

'Who did they vote for in the last election?'

'They don't vote.'

'Why?' Seigal pounced.

'My father thinks all politicians are crooks, and my mom says they're mainly hypocrites who wouldn't recognize the truth if it bit off their private parts.'

Marshall roared. 'Jerry, I love this kid.'

'What's not to love?'

They exited with Rufus at the hotel lobby, and Ty looked up at Marshall bashfully. 'Where are you going?' he said.

'To walk Rufus,' Marshall answered.

'Chris, make it quick, OK? We've got a busy morning. Ten minutes, one pee.'

'If my mom says it's OK, can I come?' Ty said to Marshall.

'Sure. Where is she?'

'She's back on twenty-two. In the Park Suite.'

'Too bad, kid,' Seigal said. 'He's in a hurry.'

'Wrong, Jerry. Rufus is in a hurry. I'm not.'

'For God's sake,' Seigal sputtered. 'What are you doing? Is this some kind of weird regression kicking in?'

'Here, take him,' Marshall said, handing him the leash.

'*What*?' Seigal's face went slack with shock and mortification. 'I don't do dogs.'

69

'You do now, Jer. Back in a minute.' To Ty he said, 'I'll go up with you. I forgot his ball.'

'Come on, Chris,' Seigal yelled. 'Who needs balls?'

Marshall threw him a dark look and Seigal added, 'Just kidding.'

On the twenty-second floor, Marshall went to the York Suite while Ty turned left and knocked on the door of the Park Suite.

'Hold on. . . .' He recognized Stephanie's voice, and then a rush of whispering. Just as Stephanie opened the door, Marshall strolled up tossing a blue ball in the air. 'This is Rufus' favorite,' he told Ty.

The maid in the open doorway was staring at him.

'Hello,' he said with a smile.

'Hello,' she replied, her voice suddenly unrecognizable to Ty, so smooth and soft. After a brief hesitation she called out, 'It's for you, ma'am.'

'What are you talking about?' Marisa looked toward the door and then froze. Ty walked into the room, grinning, followed by Assemblyman Christopher Marshall. She knew she looked stunning in Caroline Lane's white ensemble, but that was no help to her at the moment. At the moment she couldn't think of a single word to say. Her mind was a blank. Ty was supposed to be in the basement with Lily. What the hell was he doing on this floor, and of all people with Christopher Marshall, and what the hell was she doing in another woman's dress? This had to be a dream. A very bad dream.

'Hi, Ma. This is Chris. He's got this giant gray dog, Rufus, a real sweetheart of a dog – and if you say OK, I'm gonna walk with them. OK?'

'Hello,' Marshall said, clearly taken with this beautiful dark eyed, dark haired woman dressed all in white.

'Hi,' Marisa managed.

'Well?' Ty said.

'I don't know. . . .'

'Let's not forget,' Ty said, pressing his case, 'I'm a kid and I need to be outside as much as possible. You're always telling me it's important for my physical and mental well-being.'

'Well. . . .'

'Come on, Ma. A little walk.'

She felt Christopher Marshall's eyes on her; she felt their heat and was afraid to look his way.

He took that moment to step forward. He extended his hand, and his smile – she finally had to look – was dazzling. A sculptured mouth, white teeth, beautiful blue eyes, and humor and intelligence. He can win any race on looks alone, she thought.

'Chris Marshall,' he said.

She opened her mouth to answer, when Stephanie cut in, saying, 'Miss Lane. Do you want your coat?'

Marisa stared at her. 'What did you say?'

'Your coat, ma'am. The weather's so tricky this time of year.'

Marisa continued to stare at her. This deception . . . was she going to allow it to happen? It was wrong, it went against all of her instincts. What was it Stephanie had said? *It's time to feel how the other half feels.* . . .

'Weren't you just saying you wanted to stretch your legs?' Stephanie looked at her pointedly. The dare was in her eyes.

'No, I don't think so. . . .'

'If your husband wouldn't mind,' Marshall said.

'She doesn't have a husband,' Ty said, continuing to grin. He loved the way this little drama was unfolding; it took him away from his own troubles at school.

'Ty!'

'I insist then,' Marshall said. 'Come with us. If you're free.'

'Thank you, but I have. . . . I have so much to do.' Like cleaning rooms, she thought. Jesus, why can't you come right out and say it before this goes any further? What's wrong with you, girl? What are you doing?

Stephanie removed a white coat from the closet and draped it over her shoulders.

'Here we go, Miss Lane' She leaned in and tucked the price tag into the lining. She was facing the open door and saw John Bextrum, the hotel manager, heading toward the suite at a purposeful stride. She grabbed a pair of sunglasses from the front hall table and handed them to Marisa. 'You need these.' Marisa caught the urgency in her friend's tone and quickly put them on. 'Bextrum,' Stephanie whispered to her, her back to Marshall. She added in a normal tone, 'It's bright out there.'

Marshall, Marisa and Ty walked to the bank of elevators. As they arrived, the two elderly French ladies – the French poodles, Marisa thought – were chatting animatedly. An instant later, Bextrum bore down on them, hand outstretched, teeth bared in a smile. He and Marshall shook hands while Marisa crouched down by Ty, tucking in his shirt and managing to hide her face.

'This is fun,' Ty whispered.

'Be cool,' she said.

Bextrum actually wrung his hands unctuously. 'Mr Marshall, John Bextrum, hotel manager. May I offer my condolences on your father's passing? All of us here at the Beresford considered him to be part of our family – he stayed so often, you know.'

'It's very kind of you.'

'I hope you'll be making the Beresford a home away from home.'

Marshall smiled but did not reply.

When the elevator stopped at the twenty-second floor, Mr Lassiter, his wife and children piled out. Marisa turned away, hiding a grin. Mr Peter Lassiter, the notorious Romeo whose girl friend had trashed the Madison Suite yesterday, and here he was sweating and red in the face. Not a happy camper.

Mrs Lassiter said, 'I tried calling you all last night and the night before. You're not answering the pager.'

'Really? I didn't get a message.'

The younger of the Lassiter children, a tow-headed boy about eight, chanted, 'We want to go to Niketown! We want to go to Niketown!'

'Jesus,' Lassiter hissed under his breath. He looked thoroughly miserable.

Serves him right, Marisa thought. Stupid creep can't keep his mouse in the house.

The French poodles entered the elevator first, followed by Marisa, then Ty and Marshall. Finally Bextrum squeezed in and the door closed. As the elevator descended Monique and Anouk, the French poodles, inspected Marisa with their beady eyes. They spoke in French.

'Beautiful ensemble. How does she keep it clean?'

'Scotch Guard.'

'You think that's the new girl friend?'

'For tonight.'

'She's very pretty, if you like the type. A little cheap, I'd say.'

'Yes, overripe. I'd say probably Latino. Mediterranean maybe.'

'What they call Euro trash?'

'Exactly.'

They snorted laughter. Marshall turned to them with a smile and said, in virtually flawless French, with just the slightest hint of an American accent, 'Perhaps you would like to join us?'

Monique's face suddenly drained of color. 'Why don't you mind your own business?' she said.

'As you are minding yours, Madame?'

But Anouk smiled at Marshall flirtatiously. 'You speak lovely French, a rarity in this country. You did your studies at what university?'

'The cafés of Paris,' he answered.

The elevator door emitted a ding as the elevator arrived at the lobby. As the doors opened, Marshall gave a small wave.

'*Au revoir*,' he said.

'*Cochon*,' Monique growled.

Anouk smiled at Marshall and waved back coquettishly. '*Au revoir*,' she trilled.

'What was that all about?' Marisa said as the French poodles moved away.

'They said how absolutely radiant you look.'

'The chubby one seemed angry about something.'

'It's just her manner.'

Marisa and Marshall looked elegant as they crossed the vast lobby, Ty lagging a few yards behind. Heads turned and there was whispering.

John Bextrum rushed to catch up with them. 'Just one minute, miss. . . .'

Marisa froze, and so did Ty. The steady smile he had been wearing vanished.

'You dropped your scarf, Madame.'

Marisa nodded without making eye contact. He handed her the scarf, she muttered thank you, stuck it in her pocket and walked quickly through the Beresford lobby.

7

Outside the hotel Rufus was walking Jerry Seigal rather than the other way around. Seigal staggered as the huge dog pulled against the leash. When he heard a familiar voice he wanted to shrivel up and disappear. Of all the people in the world he most didn't want to see at that moment Blanton Maddox was at the top of the list, and of course it was Blanton Maddox.

'Seigal. Jerry Seigal – is that you?' Maddox, a bear of a man with pure white hair and a ruddy face, the result of years of imbibing Jameson 12-year-old whisky, hove up to the much smaller man.

Seigal's smile was more like a rictus. 'Heel or I'll kill you,' he said to Rufus under his breath. 'Hey, Blanton. Small world, eh?'

From behind Maddox appeared Marshall's adversary for the vacant senate seat, Victor Delgado. He was in his early fifties, and wiry to the point of leanness. He played two hours of tennis each day and lifted weights. His face, however, showed his age: it was shifty and feral, and his smile did nothing to soften it.

'You know Victor Delgado?' Maddox said. 'Victor – Jerry Seigal, Chris Marshall's right hand man.'

Delgado flashed an uninfectious smile. 'You groom also?'

'That's good, that's good,' Seigal said, forcing a quick laugh.

'I'm showing Victor our new building on Fifty-seventh,' Maddox said. 'Want to join us?'

'Thanks, but we're jammed.'

Maddox looked pointedly at Rufus. 'I can see that.'

As the two men walked off Delgado said, 'Don't forget to scoop.'

They laughed and receded into the crowd.

Seigal bent over Rufus and said sotto voce, 'Kill, boy, kill!'

As Marshall, Marisa and Ty were approaching the Beresford exit onto Lexington Avenue, Marshall turned to her and said, 'I should warn you. There may be some photographers out front. I can go ahead and meet you guys at the Fifty-ninth street entrance to the park.'

Marisa wasn't concerned until they walked outside into the blinding sun and the paparazzi moved in like an advancing army; she held up her hand in surprise, trying to fend off the flashes. She shrank away from them and pulled Ty with her. 'Oh my God,' she whispered.

Marshall lightly touched her arm, hoping to settle her. 'I'll handle it. Walk to the park. I'll get Rufus and we'll catch up.' He turned to the paparazzi and spoke quietly, with a smile, a small sample of the famous Marshall charm. 'Guys? There's nothing here. It's just an old friend and her son.'

'She got a name?' said a young man with a beard, a pork pie hat and two gold earrings.

'Yeah. Unidentified old friend. Tell you what, give me this and I'll give you fifteen minutes inside the benefit Monday night. Deal?'

'You'll get us in?' the young man said. 'At the Met?'

'You got it.'

Marshall looked around and an older man, also bearded, said, 'Open bar?'

'Don't push it. I'll do my best.'

Seigal, dragged by a bounding Rufus, entered the circle, puffing and out of breath. 'Chris, Chris – what are you doing?'

'I'm talking to my friends.' He winked at the paparazzi and then drew Seigal aside. He petted Rufus and said, 'Hey, boy. Did you have fun with mean old Jerry?'

'Oh, we had a great time,' Seigal said. 'Couldn't have planned it better. Blanton Maddox *and* Victor Delgado saw me walking your goddam *dog*.'

'See? It's like I've told you, Jer. You should get out more.'

He took the leash and started toward Central Park with Rufus.

'Hey Chris,' Seigal called after him, 'one o'clock. He won't be there till one-thirty. One o'clock, man!'

By the time Marisa and Ty crossed into Central Park at the southeast corner, Marshall, jogging with Rufus, caught up with them. A few pedestrians recognized him and tried to engage him in conversation, but he continued on without breaking stride, tossing off friendly 'Hi-how-are-yas?' on the fly.

'Wait up,' he called.

Marisa turned and gave him a tentative smile. 'Those photographers, all those people like hungry vultures. I couldn't do what you do. I don't see how you can.'

'You don't have a lot of choice, not in this field. You get used to it, develop a thick skin.'

'Hey Chris, can I take Rufus?' Ty said.

'Sure.'

'It's Mr Marshall, Ty.'

'No, Miss Lane. Chris is fine.'

'And you can call her Caroline,' Ty said with a grin.

'Caroline Lane,' Marshall said. 'Has a good ring to it.' He handed Ty the leash and the boy and the dog were off.

'Stay close, Ty,' Marisa said.

They stood in silence for a moment watching Ty throw the ball to Rufus who retrieved it and returned it to him.

'Thanks for this,' she said finally, breaking the brief silence. 'He's been a little down lately, and then yesterday he messed up this speech at school.'

'Speeches can be tricky. What happened?'

'I'm not sure. He froze and ran off the stage. And now he's got this thing about speaking in public. He's freaked.'

'I'm always nervous before I go on.'

She looked directly into his eyes for the first time. 'You are?'

Marshall seemed embarrassed; he brushed a hank of hair from his eyes. 'Well . . . maybe not always.'

Marisa smiled. She knew that she was attracted to this man; he was handsome, he was smart, he was kind, and she could tell he was fun to be with. She also knew that it was wrong, that attraction. It could lead nowhere, nowhere but straight to trouble. Nothing good or real could come from it. She was standing with this man in Central Park on a sun-filled day under false pretenses. She was not Caroline Lane.

She was Marisa Ventura, the Beresford maid, and every minute she spent with this man was a lie, and as the minutes piled up the lie only compounded itself. It was wrong. Wrong!

From behind them a young woman approached at a trot, three dogs pulling her along.

'Mr Marshall?'

He turned, took her and the dogs in and said, 'You're a dog walker, right?'

'Yes.'

'Don't tell me, let me guess. Mr Seigal sent you to get Rufus.'

'Yes sir.'

'Why am I not surprised?'

The girl looked toward Ty and Rufus. 'Is that him?'

Marshall nodded.

'Gee, he's really beautiful. Is it OK?'

'Is what OK?'

'If I take him back.'

'Sure. You've been hired to do that, and I hope adequately compensated.'

The girl approached Rufus, then turned back to Marshall. 'Oh, I almost forgot. This is for you. Mr Seigal said to make sure you got it.' She handed him a note.

' "Ten minutes," ' he said, reading it out loud, rolling his eyes to the heavens. 'This man never gives up.' He crumpled the note in his fist, looked around for a trash can, and not finding one stuck it in his pocket.

He and Marisa strolled over to a bench. She reached for a copy of the *New York Post* someone had abandoned and was about to slide it underneath her before preparing to sit when she noticed that the cover photo was Christopher Marshall.

'Oh look,' she said, smiling, 'I'm about to sit on your face.'

As soon as the words were out of her mouth she realized what she had said. Both of them stared straight ahead, too embarrassed to speak.

Finally Marisa broke the silence. 'Let's just . . . move on.'

'Right, perfect,' Marshall said with a nod.

They both looked at Ty who was throwing Rufus' ball up in the air and catching it.

'He seems like a terrific kid,' Marshall said.

'Thanks. I'm kind of crazy about him.'

'I can see why. I've never met a ten year old Nixon aficionado. Or maybe expert is a better word.'

'They studied the seventies last year in school. He's become obsessed with that whole period. He's the kind of kid who absorbs things – politics, music. Last month he read a biography of Henry Kissinger. On his own, not school work.'

'You're kidding. That's really remarkable.'

'He's become a historian of the nineteen-seventies. When Ty starts something he never lets up until he's looked at it from every angle. I'm waiting for him to discover another decade. Until then, I'm learning a lot.'

'I think it's great, Caroline.'

Marisa felt her body tense: Caroline Lane, the great lie. How had she ever allowed herself to get into this. 'You do?' she said, trying to remain calm.

'Yeah, I do. You two have a great relationship. I can tell.'

She smiled and they looked at each other, a lingering look that went deep. Marshall broke the spell, saying, 'So – how long are you in town for?'

'I'm . . . not sure.'

'Do you always stay at the Beresford?'

'Sometimes I feel like I live there.'

'It was my father's favorite hotel. I started staying there as a child. But, I don't know, it's a little stiff for my taste.'

'Oh.'

'What brings you to Manhattan?'

'Work.'

'What do you do?' He smiled. 'I hope I'm not asking too many questions.'

She squinted at something in the distance, then touched the sleeve of his jacket and said, 'Look – eleven o'clock, by the playground.'

'What?'

'Eleven o'clock. Check it out.'

He squinted too and spotted a paparazzi snapping away, partially camouflaged by a line of bushes.

'I know him,' Marshall said. 'Eddie Yatter. I can't seem to shake that guy.'

He got up and Marisa followed after him, the cover of the *Post* stuck to her rear end.

'What does he want?' she said.

'He works for Blanton Maddox,' Marshall answered. 'His one goal lately has been to catch me with another woman so his sleazy tabloid will say I've broken up with. . . .' He shrugged and his words trailed off.

'With your super model fiancée.'

'Not fiancée.'

Marshall suddenly noticed the page adhering to Marisa's posterior. 'I just realized that . . . ummm . . . you've got my face . . . the magazine. A piece is stuck to your . . . here, let me. . . .' He peeled it off and handed it to her. 'There you go.' He smiled awkwardly. 'Anyway – don't believe everything you read.'

'Is any of it true?'

'We were seeing each other, and now we're seeing less of each other. Much less. It's complicated.'

'Everything is complicated.'

He smiled. 'You've noticed that, haven't you?'

'Only every day of my life.'

He took her arm. 'Come on – follow me.'

Marisa called out to Ty, who ambled over to them, still throwing the ball into the air. 'I'm the world's worst athlete,' he told Marshall. 'I'm always picked last for the team, so I'm practicing pop ups.'

'Good idea.'

'I'm catching more balls than I'm dropping. Of course I don't have any audience.'

'Rufus would be proud of you.'

They walked a few hundred yards farther into Central Park to a rocky outcropping. To the west the skyline was spread out blue and vast.

'Two different worlds,' Marisa said. 'The bustle in the streets just a minute away – and then this.'

'Interesting perspective, isn't it? And best of all, it's Yatter free ... at least for the moment.' His eyes followed hers, across the park to the west. 'You know when I come here the most? When I have to give a speech and I get nervous.'

Ty looked at him sharply. 'You get nervous?'

'Sure. I break out in a sweat. My hands shake.'

'See that?' Marisa said, giving Ty a squeeze.

'I don't know about you,' Marshall said to the boy, 'but sometimes when I get in front of people my heart starts to race and I can't remember my words. Everything becomes a blur.'

Ty juggled Rufus' ball between his hands in excitement. 'I can't believe that happens to you, Chris. The exact same thing happens to me.'

'And in my business that's not such a good thing, right?'

'Right, yeah. You have to communicate with the public and sell yourself at the same time. So what do you do?'

Marshall reached into his pocket and pulled out a twisted paperclip. He showed it to Ty. 'I hold onto this while I'm speaking.'

Ty held out a hand, but Marshall quickly put it back in his pocket.

'A paperclip. Was that a paperclip?'

'You see, I needed to find something to draw all the nervous energy away from my heart. That's the function of the paper-clip.'

Ty nodded, his face pinched in concentration. 'Sort of like a lightning rod?'

'Exactly. Everything goes into the paperclip, and what's left are my words.'

'Your speech,' Ty said, nodding.

'You've got it. A very smooth, and I'd like to think compelling speech.'

Marshall winked at Marisa, who winked back. She was enjoying this by-play between her son and Christopher Marshall. It was as though she had waked up this Saturday morning to ordinary reality only to be thrust into the heart of a dream.

'Some of the best speakers in the world use the paperclip method,' Marshall confided to Ty in a whisper. 'Henry Kissinger, for instance.'

Ty frowned and gave Marshall a close look. 'Kissinger

wasn't known for his speaking ability.'

'Then imagine what he would have been like without this. . . .' Again he fished out the paperclip and dangled it in front of the boy.

'Just a simple paperclip,' Ty said, a note of awe in his voice.

'Maybe not so simple after all. And listen, I don't want to read about this in tomorrow's papers.'

'I won't say anything. I swear.' Ty hesitated, his eyes trained on the ball as he squeezed it. 'You're not putting me on, are you?'

'I'm not putting you on.'

'Because people try to do that to me at school all the time. For an intelligent person I'm slightly gullible.'

'This is on the level, Ty.'

'Will any paperclip do the trick?'

'You have to try it to see. Experiment around.'

Marisa reached for Ty's hand. 'So you'll try again?' she said.

'I don't know. I might lose my way. Just like yesterday.'

'But you might not,' Marshall said. 'And if you do, big deal. Nobody's perfect. My dad used to say, If you don't give yourself a second chance how can you expect anyone else to?'

Marisa ruffled Ty's hair. 'Chris' father sounds like a pretty smart man.'

'He was,' Marshall said, a shadow falling across his features. 'He was great. He always gave me about fifty chances to be better, and eventually I figured it out.' He turned to Ty. 'So . . . we straight on the paperclip?'

'Ty? He's talking to you.'

The boy looked up at Marshall, his expression serious and determined. 'I'm straight on that,' he said.

'Good man.'

'Hey, Chris,' Ty said, 'I've got an idea. Let's go see the penguins in the zoo.'

Marisa looked hard at him. 'We really have to be getting back.'

'Just a few minutes, Ma.'

'Yeah,' Marshall said, smiling. 'Just a few minutes.'

They walked to the zoo and watched the penguins swim in their icy world behind thick glass.

'Look at those guys go!' Ty cried. 'Woooooooweeeee!'

Marisa and Marshall laughed.

'They look like they're wearing tuxedos, don't they?' Marisa said. 'Little waddling men. All dressed up with no place to go.'

'Speaking of which,' Marshall said, 'there's this thing I have to go to Monday night. Black tie, twenty-five hundred a plate. Plenty of waddling men in tuxedos.'

She turned to him and he was looking intently at the penguins. 'Twenty-five hundred? I hope you get to keep the plate. What's it for?'

'It's an inner city literacy campaign,' Marshall explained. 'A big, big event, attracting the city's social heavy hitters. Blandon Maddox throws it every year. Trying to legitimize himself.'

'Maddox? The guy who hired that creep Yatter to get pictures of us?'

'One and the same.'

'I don't get it. Why would you go?'

'Exposure.' He looked uncomfortable. 'Jerry Seigal, my chief of staff, he thinks it's important for me to be seen there.'

'Won't everyone know you're there just to . . . expose your-self?'

Marshall's laughter, a high pitched, infectious giggle, forced Marisa to join him.

'Well, when you put it that way. . . .'

'Uh uh – *you* put it that way. And I don't care how much these people are paying for dinner. You shouldn't have to serve yourself to them no matter what the cause.'

'Let's not beat around the bush here. Why don't you tell me what you *really* think?'

'You're making fun of me.'

'No I'm not. I really want to know.'

She regarded him seriously for a moment. 'OK – you want to know what I think? I think if this Maddox guy wants to do some good, why not just give the twenty-five hundred per plate to the inner city schools and everybody eat a little lighter? You know what I'm saying?'

'Good point. I have a great idea. You come with me, Caroline, and tell him yourself.'

Again she stiffened at the mention of the name Caroline. 'Monday?' she said, watching Ty toss Rufus' ball in the air and try unsuccessfully to catch it behind his back. 'I . . . I'm busy. Sorry.'

'Sorry you're busy Monday,' Marshall said softly, 'or sorry, you're busy period.'

She forced herself to look at him. 'It's complicated.'

'What isn't?'

She shook her head. 'Very complicated.'

'Got it. Say no more.'

'Listen, we've got to bolt. Ty – c'mon, we're gonna be late.'

'Late for what?'

'*Late,*' she said, glaring at him.

As the three of them stood at the zoo exit by the famous

animal clock, Marshall said, 'I can't believe it. Here we are in the park and we haven't even seen the snakes – other than Yatter.'

'The guy taking pictures? He should be caged.'

'Good one, Ty,' Marshall said approvingly. 'You couldn't be more right.'

Marisa smiled, and her tone held a note of finality. 'It was really nice to meet you, Chris Marshall. You're different than I thought you'd be. I mean, not that I thought about you, but you know, if one was wondering about you they wouldn't guess that you were . . . I mean. . . .' She laughed nervously. 'Oh my God, I don't know what I'm saying. Ty, c'mon now.' She grabbed his hand.

'You're not like anyone I know either,' Marshall said.

'Yes I am. I'm just like everyone else. Wherever you look you'll see me.'

'I don't believe that.'

'Well, that's nice. Goodbye now.'

She pulled on Ty's jacket, but he lingered, looking at Marshall.

'I have something for you, Ty.' Marshall reached into his jacket pocket and handed the boy a bunch of paperclips. 'Try them out. Find a few you like, but don't use them all on one speech, OK?'

'OK.'

Ty pocketed the paperclips and gave the Assemblyman a restrained high five, which he returned. Marisa was trying to drag Ty away, but he continued to resist her.

'What about Rufus' ball?'

'Return it later. Rufus will be glad to see you.'

'Thanks for the paperclips, Chris,' Ty said over his shoulder. 'And keep up the good voting record.'

'I'll do my best,' Marshall said. 'You're my conscience.'

As he watched mother and son exit the zoo he tried to understand what he was feeling. He only knew that whatever it was, it was something he had never felt before.

8

Marisa walked stealthily through the lobby, head averted from the front desk, and then rushed to the locker room in the basement. She called Stephanie's cell phone number and said, 'Where are you?'

'The kitchen.'

'Come to the locker room now.'

A moment later, Stephanie came running in and helped Marisa step out of the Dolce and Gabbana outfit.

'He invited me to this gala dinner on Monday,' Marisa said. 'Twenty-five hundred bucks a plate. Can you believe it?'

'And you accepted, right?'

'I didn't. I told him things are complicated.'

'*Complicated*? Are you nuts? What kind of an answer is that?'

'Honest,' Marisa said. 'My name happens to be Marisa Ventura, *not* some rich bitch Caroline Lane. I feel like a complete fraud.'

'The only complicated thing between me and him would be unhooking my bra strap.'

'You're such a slut.'

'Yes, and I'm proud of it.'

As Marisa carefully pulled the tunic over her head she said, 'What am I supposed to do? Make his bed with me in it? Get real, Steph. He thinks I'm a guest here, one of his people, not some maid. What do you suppose he'd say if he found out the truth? Probably have me fired. I wouldn't blame him.'

'OK, OK, enough with that already. Tell me what he's like.'

'Sexy eyes.'

'Yeah?'

'Nice lips. Nicely shaped.'

'Umm hmmm. How about the hands. Big?'

'Perfect. Slender, sensitive, long fingers.'

Stephanie nodded. 'Perfect works.'

'Long legs. Slender. A great smile.'

'Stop it. You're making me hot.'

Suddenly they heard Paula Burns' raspy voice yelling, 'Marisa? *Marisa Ventura. Are you back there?*'

'Yes, ma'am,' she called out. She whispered to Stephanie, 'Damn, she must know something. Help me.'

Stephanie pulled her maid's uniform down over her head as Marisa whipped off her suede pants. She did up the buttons on her uniform, fingers flying, as Stephanie stuffed the clothes in her locker. She slammed it shut just as Paula Burns rounded the corner.

'What are you doing?' she said, scoping out the room with her beady eyes that never missed anything, especially any irregularity.

'I just, ah, spilled something on my uniform. I had to change.'

'Well, Mr Bextrum wants to see you in his office. In ten minutes.'

After she left, Marisa looked at Stephanie, biting her lower lip and shaking her head.

'Do you get the feeling the yogurt is just about to hit the fan?'

When Christopher Marshall sauntered into the York Suite twenty minutes later, whistling and seemingly without a care in the world, Seigal immediately cornered him. Lionel was supervising two maids in the cleaning up. With a glance at the head butler Seigal said, 'They should've been out of here an hour ago. The regular maid seems to have taken a powder.'

'No big deal, Jer. You're going to work yourself into an early grave. There are important details and then there are details you don't sweat over. Sometimes I don't think you know the difference.'

'OK, friend,' Seigal said gravely. 'Let's zero in on an important detail. Delgado *killed* while you walked the goddam dog. This day so far is a wash out, and at the moment an early grave doesn't sound like a bad idea.'

Marshall was patting his jacket pockets, barely listening. 'You got a pen?' he said.

Seigal handed him a gold Mark Cross pen and said sarcastically, 'Sure, Chris, anything else I can do to make myself useful?'

Marshall grabbed a notepad from the desk, scribbled something and rushed through the suite to the bedroom.

'Lionel,' he said. 'That's your name, isn't it?'

'Yes sir.'

'I've got to get this note to the woman in the Park Suite. Her name is Caroline Lane. Can you handle that for me?'

'Right away, sir.'

'Thank you.'

As Lionel departed, Seigal said, 'What are you doing? Who's Caroline Lane in the Park Suite? Should I know?'

'Just someone I met,' Marshall said casually. 'You wanted me to have an escort for that Maddox thing Monday night. Well, I've got one.'

'Yeah, but I was thinking more along the lines of a blind, ex-illiterate Republican senior citizen who learned to read while fighting the Nazis.'

'I thought your mother was in Florida.'

'Funny. Funnnnay. So what's with this Lane dame?'

'Gorgeous. Interesting. Very bright.'

'Well, she better not be married, on drugs or a Democrat.'

Marshall shrugged.

'Chris. Hel*lo*? I'm talking to you. You checked her out, didn't you? *Didn't you?*'

'You're hyperventilating again, Jer.'

'Jesus!' Seigal rushed up to an aide in the living room, grabbed the cell phone from his ear and whispered, 'Find out what you can on the woman in the Park Suite . . . Caroline Lane. Pronto!'

Marisa stood at the open door to John Bextrum's office, her heart hammering, her mouth dry with fear. Maybe Caroline Lane had returned to the Park Suite unexpectedly and discovered that her clothes were missing. Maybe some-

94

one had seen her in Caroline Lane's fancy outfit parading up Fifth Avenue and had ratted on her. Whatever it was, it couldn't be good. If they fired her she would have to scramble fast for a new job; like most of her friends Marisa lived from paycheck to paycheck. There was no slack; she had to stretch every penny. Marcus helped out sporadically, but he wasn't very generous with the amounts he doled out. Maybe she had made a mistake when she had refused alimony and child support at the time of the divorce. 'Pride,' her mother had told her, but she was the one who had initiated the divorce and she hadn't wanted to be beholden to Marcus in any way. She had been determined to stand on her own two feet, be her own woman, independent and free. She could hear her mother now: 'Pride cometh before a fall. . . .'

As she waited at the door for Bextrum to notice her and invite her in, he said to Paula Burns, 'So . . . we'll keep an eye on Lionel Bloch.'

'There's a rumor he has a drinking problem,' Burns said.

'He's been a good employee for many years.'

'But his work is falling off, John.'

'We'll keep a close eye on him.'

Bextrum looked up and saw Marisa. He nodded for her to come in as Burns was saying, 'You know, yesterday he cut himself.'

He waved her remark away. 'Later. . . .' With a polished smile he said, 'Miss Ventura, please take a seat.'

Burns stepped back from his desk, but did not leave.

'I assume you know why we've called you here.' He switched to his serious expression; his repertoire of expressions was both narrow and predictable.

Marisa took a deep breath and said in a small voice, 'I think so. Yes.'

'Do you know what the foundation for a great hotel is?' he asked, leaning forward.

'Um. Location?'

Bextrum shook his head. 'Loyalty and trust. Would you say that those are qualities you possess?'

She searched his eyes, looking for a clue to her fate. But there was nothing to read in his eyes – no sign, not a clue. 'I would,' she said after a slight hesitation. 'Yes sir.'

'Miss Burns here happens to agree with you, and she has urged me to consider your application.'

'Sir?'

'We had no idea you were interested in management until Miss Kehoe brought us your application first thing this morning. Yours is the only one we have received thus far, and I must say, it's most impressive.'

'Oh.' Marisa was too stunned to utter a coherent sentence.

'By the way,' Burns said, 'you forgot your social security number. We have it on record, of course, but you should fill in the blanks. Also your mother's maiden name. If you could just fill those in and sign.'

Marisa looked at Paula Burns, who was actually smiling at her.

'You're considering me?'

'We most definitely are,' Bextrum answered for Burns. 'To be fair, we have to look at other applications as they come in, but as I said, we're most impressed.'

'A maid applying,' Burns said, 'is most unusual. It shows great initiative.'

96

'If you are chosen,' Bextrum went on, 'we would normally expect you to go through the entire program and then train for a full year as a valet. But circumstances at present are rather extraordinary due to overbooking and understaffing. So if you're selected, Miss Ventura, you will be moved directly into management after the six week training period. With the proviso, of course, that you pass the practical exam and fulfill the requirements of each station.'

A smile was pasted on Marisa's face, locked there, beyond her control. 'I'm very surprised,' she managed to say, 'and flattered.'

'No need to feel flattered,' Paula Burns said. 'You've earned your chance.'

'We should have a decision within ten days,' Bextrum said as he escorted Marisa out of his office. 'So you see, when one door closes, a window opens. Do you understand what I mean by that?'

'I'm not sure, Mr Bextrum,' she said. In fact she didn't have a clue.

'He means,' Burns said, 'that this door is your window.'

'So jump!' Bextrum said.

Marisa shrank away and gave him a wan smile.

'Just a little in-house joke,' Bextrum said. 'Good luck.'

Marisa burst into the bathroom and approached the one stall with the door closed. She knew Stephanie's habits. The smoke alarm was dangling from the ceiling, disarmed, and a haze of smoke hung in the air. That meant that her friend, one of the few smokers on the staff and the only one daring enough to take this kind of chance, given the iron rule of

Bextrum and Burns, would surely be in there.

'Steph?' She pounded on the door. 'Open up.'

'Don't tell me you're busted.'

'No, *you* are.' She banged on the door again. 'Open up.'

'Why should I? You sound pissed.'

'I am pissed. Unlock.'

Stephanie slid open the catch. She was sitting on the closed toilet lid smoking a filtered Camel. 'What's your problem, girl?'

Marisa waved away the smoke. 'You had no right to do that.'

'Do what?'

'*You* know. Don't play little Miss Innocent with me. You filled out an application for me and sent it in. What the hell were you thinking?'

Stephanie broke into a wide grin. 'Hey, are they really considering you? That's fan*tas*tic. I knew they would, I just *knew* it.'

'What gives you the right to put my name on something and pass it off as mine? I just can't understand you sometimes. Freaking unguided missile.'

'But I did you a favor.'

'You want to do me another favor?' Marisa said, blowing the smoke away from her face. 'From now on, mind your own friggin' business. Stay out of mine.'

She closed the stall door with a slam and marched into the locker room. She sat on the bench, holding her head in her hands. Too much was happening to her and she felt dizzy, light in the head. First I'm masquerading as a guest, pretending to be someone I'm not, then I go walking in Central Park with Christopher Marshall, *the* Christopher

Marshall, when I'm supposed to be on duty. Pretending to be someone I'm not, maybe even flirting a little with the man. Then Bextrum calls me into his office and instead of firing me, practically offers me a job in management. Too much – *too much*. . . . Her head was whirling. She felt a hand on her shoulder. She looked up to see Stephanie standing over her.

'OK, you're mad at me, Maris. I guess you've got a right, but I think you're wrong. For two years you've been yapping about getting out of uniform, all the ideas you've got, etcetera, etcetera. I'm thinking, why? Why isn't my girl walking the walk? Then yesterday I'm having coffee with Rosalie from Personnel. I ask her – "what if Marisa applies for Christina's old position, does she have a shot?" and she goes, "Marisa who?" and I go, "Marisa Ventura, she's applying," and Rosalie goes, "If she applies I'll slip it to the top of the pile, you know what I'm sayin'?". So I act real nonchalant like and I go, "Hasn't she ever applied for the management program before?" So she checks it out and tells me you've never put your name in for anything. . . .' The two women stared at each other in silence. 'Marisa?'

'What?'

'You lied to me, girl. My best friend lied to me. Last year you said you filled out an application for valet training.'

'I was going to.'

'But you didn't.'

'I figured, what's the point? What chance do I have? There are many more qualified people.'

'Spoken like your mother. Always ready to put yourself down.'

'Well, maybe she's right.'

'Sure, and maybe she isn't. And I happen to think she isn't. Plus, I think something else. I think maybe you're just too chicken shit to make a move on your own. That's why I went ahead and did it myself. That way, if they took you you'd be happy, and if they didn't, you'd never know the difference. So sue me. . . .'

She sat beside Marisa on the bench and reached for her hand. She said softly, 'We only get so many chances, people like you and me. We have to grab 'em when they come. These are the golden years, Maris, and they pass by so damn fast. This is when we have to prove our mothers wrong. Don't waste 'em.'

'But what if our mothers are right, Steph?'

'There's only one way to find out,' Stephanie said. 'You got to have the guts to take the next step.' She kissed her friend on the cheek and rose from the bench. 'Back to the grind for this girl. The Jefferson Suite calls.'

'Cutler still there? The Mafia sharpy?'

' 'Fraid so. He hasn't put a move on me yet, though.'

Marisa sat for a moment staring at her locker, but instead of her locker she saw a whole new life beginning to unfold. She was both thrilled and terrified.

As Marisa was punching out at the end of the day, Keef was absently scanning his monitors.

'Anything juicy, Keef?'

'Can't say there is. The action be slow. Nobody stealin' kisses in the corridor or robbin' the carts.'

'Too bad.'

'But speakin' of action,' he said with a sly grin, 'it was some day you had, huh?'

'What do you mean?'

His smile grew wider. 'We got a sayin' in Jamaica – the higher the monkey climbs, the more she gets exposed. You get my drift?'

'Keef – how come you know so much?'

'Well . . . bein' God and all. . . .'

'Yeah?' she said, smiling.

'And also, bein' the monitor man.' He shrugged and suddenly looked serious. 'Be careful, Marisa.'

'OK, Keef. I'll try.'

'Night now.'

'Night, God.'

On their way home, Marisa and Ty stopped for a bag of Chinese take-out food. Ty had kept up a steady conversation on the subway ride home, but Marisa had been unusually quiet. As they approached their building, through the raucous sounds of street corner philosophers, rummies and kids running wild in the streets, she turned to Ty and said, 'What we did today was wrong.'

'But you didn't really lie, Ma. Not technically.'

'Technically doesn't cut it with me. Letting someone believe something is true when it's not, that's as much a lie as a lie is. You see what I mean?'

'You didn't do anything bad.'

'I let him think I was staying in the Park Suite, not cleaning it. I'm the maid, Ty.'

'Ma, I hate to break it to you, but I don't think he's after your money.'

Marisa smiled. 'Reach into my pocket and take my keys.'

Ty fished for them.

'Unlock the door. Hurry! This food is hot.'

At nine-thirty Marisa tucked Ty into bed. She hugged him. 'How did I get such a great kid?' she said.

'Because you have a great mother,' he answered.

She broke the hug and looked at him.

'That's what Abuela says.'

'Well, I guess Abuela's right.' She fussed with his blanket, positioning it just so, with the top sheet overlapping the blanket by precisely four inches. 'So for right now, with the review and everything – you know, the management position – we gotta be extra careful. And that means no Chris Marshall.'

'Why? It's not like you're breaking some law.'

'Ty! If you see him. . . .' She let the threat hang in the air.

'Don't worry, I'll run and hide. I'll make myself invisible, like that lady says you all should be.'

'Paula Burns.'

'The witch.' He was silent for a moment, staring up at his mother. 'But I have to tell you, Ma. He does like you.'

'How do you know?'

'I know.'

'Well, that's nice, but it doesn't mean anything.'

'I don't know. You're always telling me I have a sixth sense about things.'

'Not about this you don't. Now go to sleep.'

'Will you sing our song?'

'No.'

'Come on. First and last verses, please.'

'OK – that's it.' She snuggled on the bed with him and began singing 'The First Time I Ever Saw Your Face,' giving

it her best Roberta Flack imitation. By the time she reached
the second verse Ty was fast asleep.

9

Marisa slept poorly that night. Christopher Marshall kept breaking in and troubling her dreams. They were having cocktails in the lounge at the Beresford dressed only in bathing suits and next they were standing at a fish market in Jamaica with Keef and Chris was feeding her oysters from the open shells and next they were riding the Wonder Wheel at Coney Island, sitting in one of the chairs with runners that seemed to sling them off into eternity at the top of each revolution. He was kissing her. . . . She was returning his kisses. . . . She would awake, drink water, then fall back into the continuing dream.

She was edgy in the morning and had to restrain herself from snapping at Ty.

When they arrived at the Beresford, Keef set Ty up on a stool beside him in his booth as Marisa punched in. Keef had a newspaper out on the table in front of him, the Sunday *Daily News*, and Marisa did a double take when she saw the front page. She studied it quickly, then said to Keef, 'Can I borrow this?'

'You can have it. I read my fill on the train. Murder, rapes, financial double-dealings and the strange doin's of movie stars. Have mercy, what a world we live in.' He winked. 'But there's a pretty good story right there on the front.'

'Thanks, Keef.' She blew Ty a kiss and said, 'See ya later, honey.' She slipped the paper into her tote bag and hurried along to the morning briefing. When that broke up, she pulled Stephanie aside.

'Did you see this?'

On the front page was a photograph of Christopher Marshall, Marisa and Rufus the day before, with Ty in the extreme background, his back to the camera. The caption read: DOG DAY AFTERNOON.

Stephanie studied it and grinned.

'Yeah. So? The gentleman is some hunk all right.'

Marisa pointed to herself. 'What if Bextrum sees this? Or Burns? This is awful – a nightmare.'

'I hate to burst your bubble, sweetie, but you can't even tell it's you. Your face is hidden—'

'*Partly* hidden—'

'Enough. You're not recognizable. Don't worry about it.'

'I think Keef recognized me.'

'Yes, but Keef sees everything. He has the gift.'

'It's on the front page, Steph. *The front page*. I'm there for the whole world to see.'

'Would you stop it? Jesus, you do one spontaneous thing in your life and you think you're going to hell.' She handed back the paper. 'Don't be so Catholic – please. You only live once, you know.'

As they walked to their carts Marisa nodded. 'I do know that. And my intention is to do it right.'

★

On the level above, in the Beresford coffee shop, Christopher Marshall was having a power breakfast with three supporters when Jerry Seigal marched in, clearly agitated and making little effort to hide it. He held a newspaper and waved it like a baton as he spoke.

'Hello, gentlemen, everything all right? The omelets are delicious here.' He shot daggers at Marshall through a thin smile. 'I need to pull our candidate away for just a moment. I'm sorry. I'll return him quickly and in good condition.'

Seigal walked to the far end of the restaurant, next to an empty booth, and Marshall joined him there.

'What's wrong with you, Jer? You're twitching.'

Seigal shoved the paper under his nose.

'*This. This* is what's wrong with me.'

Marshal stared at the photograph and broke into a chuckle. "Dog Day Afternoon." Pretty clever headline for a stupid tabloid.'

'Listen to me now.'

'What choice do I have?'

'You know what this is going to cost me? Do you have any idea? An entire day of doing nothing but covering your ass. I've already gotten calls from *The Washington Post*, *The New York Times*, *The Chicago Sun*, some others, demanding information. I'm ducking questions about her identity, her background, who the kid is. Just when we get them to focus on your assets, they're focusing on hers. Thanks, Chris. Thanks for nothing.'

'For God's sake, man, lighten up. Her assets are fantastic, don't you think?'

Seigal glared at him and shook his head. 'Sometimes I wonder about you.'

107

'That's funny. Sometimes I wonder about me too.'

He smiled and returned to his table.

Marisa and Stephanie approached the Adams Suite together. The Suite was Stephanie's assignment, but Marisa had come along in case the strange guest happened to make one of his appearances. Stephanie had been entertaining the other maids with tales of Randolph Simmons' antics for a week.

'Remember,' Stephanie cautioned, 'just keep your cool. He's a Full Monty. Yesterday in a two-hour span he exposed himself to me three times.'

'Accidentally on purpose, right?'

'You got it. It's always, "Oh, I'm so sorry, I didn't know you were here." Pathetic.'

Marisa sighed. 'I'll be glad when he's gone.'

'Who? The Full Monty? He's not yours.'

'No. Chris Marshall.'

'Oh, hello? Nice to see you're with me here.'

'Sorry. I just got a lot on my mind.'

'You still pissed at me for handing in the application?'

'I guess not. It's done now.'

'You know what I think? A little bird tells me you've fallen in love with the guy.'

'What does it matter?'

'Exactly. Have you seen what he goes out with?' She whistled. 'Ritzy, ritzy.' She reached into her cart and pulled out a copy of *Cosmo*. The super model Daniella Von Graas was reclining, most scantily, on the cover. 'Daniella Von Graas, the Dutch treat. I carted this around all day yesterday meaning to show it to you.'

'They broke up.'

'Oh honey. How naïve can you get? Maybe I can show you some lovely swamp land in Florida.'

'They did. He told me.'

'OK – who cares? I mean, get real. He was terrific to take a walk in the park with, but you need to focus on the bigger picture here.' She held Marisa's face in two hands and drew her close. 'You heard Lionel after our briefing. You got a chance, Maris, it's all along the grapevine this morning. A maid in management! A first! Busting straight through the glass ceiling.'

'We'll see.'

Stephanie's expression turned serious. 'Just remember one thing, yesterday was a fluke. You mixed with a guy from the Suave Bola crowd, you had a few laughs, a bit of a flirtation. It's done. And I'm real proud of you for doing it. But today is back to reality.' She picked up toilet bowl cleaner and held it under Marisa's nose. '*This* is our reality.' She walked toward the bathroom. 'You gotta wash that man right outta your bowl.'

At that moment a naked Randolph Simmons – blond, plump, virtually hairless – came out of the bathroom. He stared at Stephanie and Marisa, feigning surprise.

'Oh!' he said in soft, self-loving tenor tones. 'I had no idea someone was here. So sorry.'

'Sure you didn't,' Stephanie said. 'Ain't that funny how it just keeps happening? Over and over and over? A big fat coincidence, right?' She tossed him a towel. 'Don't worry, Mr Monty – er, Mr Simmons – no big deal. And I mean *no big deal.*'

'Later, Steph,' Marisa said, edging toward the door. She ran down the corridor choking back laughter.

She wheeled her cart to the Park Suite and knocked softly. 'Housekeeping,' she said. When there was no reply she inserted her passkey in the lock and entered. In the living room, on the floor, sat Caroline Lane and a friend in leotards, pretzeled up with 'magic circle' tensioners squeezed between their knees in a Pilates exercise. Both women were grunting loudly. Their trainer, a wiry man in his early forties, stood over them frowning with concentration.

'Squeezing now,' he said, 'radiating out from the pelvis.'

'I'm sorry,' Marisa said. 'I'll come back.'

'That's OK,' Caroline Lane said through clenched teeth. 'Work around us.'

The other woman, an older brunette carbon copy of Caroline, gave Marisa a cool glance. 'We could use towels, *por favor.*'

'Yes, ma'am,' Marisa said. She took extra towels from the cart.

'Squeezing,' the trainer said, with a trace of impatience. '*Squeezing.*'

The two women grunted with effort, and Caroline, tight and awkward, was having trouble following instructions.

'. . . And slowly . . . slowly . . . releasing. . . .'

Caroline's 'magic circle' became unmoored and went flying, just missing Marisa.

'Oh hell!' Caroline cried, breathing quickly, hyperventilating.

'You OK?' the other woman said.

Caroline Lane shook her head, staring down at the floor. Marisa handed the 'magic circle' back to the trainer and placed towels by the equipment.

'Here, Caroline,' the trainer said, handing her the 'magic circle,' but she waved it away. She shook her head and tears rolled down her cheeks.

'What is it?' her friend said. She reached out and lifted Caroline's chin. 'Honey? Is it Eric?'

Caroline Lane nodded. 'He hasn't called me once,' she said, speaking in a series of sobs and sighs. 'Not *once*, Rachel, not my cell, not my service, not the hotel. So last night I said, Oh what the hell. I called him – you know, a moment of weakness, maybe the wine – oh, how I regret that. And he was with . . . oh, never mind. I can't . . . I just can't deal with it.'

'You feel too much,' her friend told her. 'He takes advantage of you. That's just like a man.'

The trainer stood over the two women, hands on hips, one foot tapping. 'Shall we do some band work, ladies?'

Rachel nodded and fastened a long rubber band around her ankles. 'Go on,' she said to Caroline. 'I'm listening.'

The trainer stretched the band over her legs into a wide V.

'I heard her in the background yapping away, the bitch!'

'The dancer you call cheap wine?'

'I think so. If not, it's something cheap. You can depend on that, knowing Eric. It could've been his ex.'

'Cheap too.'

'Oh is she ever!'

'We have work to do, ladies,' the trainer said, no longer attempting to hide his impatience.

There was a discreet knock on the door and Lionel entered.

'Butler service, Ms Lane,' he said.

'Not now!' Rachel shouted at him. 'Can't you see we're busy?'

Lionel gave her a level glance and addressed Caroline

111

Lane. 'I have a message from Mr Christopher Marshall.'

Rachel suddenly shot up to a sitting position. 'Christopher Marshall?' She turned to Caroline, who was busy wiping her eyes with her knuckles like a child. 'As in *the* Christopher Marshall?'

Caroline also rose to a sitting position, her red-rimmed eyes fastened intently on Lionel.

'Mr Marshall is staying in the York Suite,' he said. 'He's wondering if you have a response to the luncheon invitation placed in your room yesterday.'

Rachel turned to the trainer. 'We're through, Russ,' she barked out. 'We're done. Thank you.'

'He left it in the room?' Caroline said to Lionel.

The trainer, ignoring Rachel, said to Caroline, 'I'll have to charge you for the full hour.'

'Yes,' Lionel answered. 'It was left yesterday.'

'Fine,' Rachel told the trainer.

'One hour for each of you,' he said, leveling a cool glance at her.

'*Fine*. Now get out.'

'For lunch?' Caroline said, her voice suddenly stronger.

'That's correct.'

'White trash,' Rachel muttered, watching the trainer flounce out of the suite.

'Where?' Caroline said.

'Madame?'

'Where is the lunch?'

'In his suite.'

Rachel leaned toward Caroline and kissed her cheek, or rather the air approximately an inch from her cheek. 'You see, sweetie? There is a God.'

Caroline continued to stare at Lionel, a quizzical expression tightening her features as though she didn't quite believe him. But this couldn't be an elaborate hoax, not if the butler were involved.

'Shall I give him an answer?' Lionel said.

Caroline was speechless.

'Yes,' Rachel answered for her. 'Tell him yes! What time?'

'One o'clock, Madame.'

Marisa, busy dusting, detected an ironic note in his use of the word. She suppressed a smile.

'She'll be there,' Rachel said. 'Thank you ever so much.' She waved him away.

Lionel bowed his way out.

Rachel sprang to her feet and pulled Caroline to hers.

'How did this happen, Caroline? Tell Rachel all!'

'We met at a thing in Southampton last summer. I *thought* we had a moment.' She read the invitation in wonder. '. . . .Steal away an hour, please. . . .'

'How cute. Do you think he saw you in the hall?'

'Who cares? What should I wear?' Caroline was hopping up and down in her excitement like a child.

Marisa, having finished cleaning the bathroom, was hugging the wall on her way out, hoping to leave unnoticed.

'Maria?' Caroline called after her. 'Do me a favor, please? Urgent.'

'Ma'am?'

'Run downstairs and get those outfits you returned for me yesterday.' She turned to Rachel, saying, 'There's this divine Dolce cashmere coat. . . .'

Marisa spoke hesitantly. 'They're still in the front hall closet.' Over Caroline's raised eyebrow, she quickly added, 'I

... thought you might want a second look.'

Caroline's expression immediately brightened; she rushed to the closet and pulled out the coat, holding it close to her body, twisting back and forth as though modeling it.

'Oh you're good!' she said to Marisa. 'You should be a personal assistant. You really should.'

Rachel compressed her lips in a frown. 'She's a maid, Caroline.'

'So are personal assistants,' Caroline said. 'Just better titles.'

Not looking at either of them, Marisa said, 'Actually, I'm under review for a management position here.'

Caroline ignored her comment as she unzipped the garment bag. 'What do you think, Rach? Gucci pants, Dolce coat? Or Ralph Lauren skirt, Manolo pumps?'

'They're all divine. . . .'

Caroline held the various outfits to her body, her face flushed with excitement.

'Let me see,' Rachel said, squinting as she evaluated her friend. 'OK – the pants, open sandals, see-through blouse, colored bra. Carry the Dolce coat – just for effect. You'll be a knockout.'

Marisa noticed that this Rachel bitch was wearing a see-through blouse with a colored bra.

Caroline turned to her. 'Maria?'

'Huh?'

'For God's sake,' Rachel said. 'She barely speaks English.'

'Cow,' Marisa said under her breath in Spanish.

Rachel stared hard at her. 'What did you say?'

'Excuse me?'

'Come on, Maria,' Caroline said. 'What do you think?'

114

Marisa, who had locked expressions with Rachel, looked away. She said, 'That beige beaded skirt, and maybe that crocheted halter you have hanging in the closet. Casual, sexy. No stockings, and I'd definitely eighty-six that coat. It sends the wrong message – looks like you're making too big a deal about a lunch date – a little too eager to please.' She continued to study Caroline Lane, her head inclined to the side. 'Oh, and by the way, that see-through blouse and colored bra number? To me it reads a little like an older gal, desperate, trying too hard, don't you think?' She shot a quick glance at Rachel, then back to Caroline. 'Make him work for it.'

'For God's *sake*, Caroline,' Rachel said. 'Are you going to listen to her?'

'Thank you, Maria,' Caroline said. 'You can go now. I can see you're in a hurry.'

'Ma'am,' she said, and left.

Caroline whirled around to Rachel, her eyes bright with excitement.

'I have two words for you, Rachel Hoffberg. Eric who?' She laughed. 'You know something strange and wonderful? The name Eric no longer even rings a bell.'

10

fter Marisa took a short break to check on Ty – he was
sitting with Keef raptly watching the various monitors, soaking up life in the Beresford ('It's like a
three-ring circus, Ma,' he told her, 'only the animals are the
rich human types') – she hurried to the twenty-second floor
pantry and helped Lionel with his inventory. She wrote down
items as he called them out, 'two cases Perrier, beverage
napkins, two packs, coffee, one case regular, one case decaf,'
and when he finished the inventory he said, 'Mark the shift,
Miss Ventura. Date it and sign it.' She did and handed it to
him.

He gave her a brief nod. 'Review your protocols. For table
setting and wine service,' he said. 'We're serving luncheon in
the York Suite.'

She drew in a sharp breath and a flicker of alarm pinched
her features. She had to resist the urge to cross herself. 'We
are?'

He looked at her sharply. 'Are you all right?'

She swallowed and said, 'Yes, of course,' and forced a smile
to show that she meant it.

When they entered the York Suite, Marisa was relieved that
Christopher Marshall was nowhere to be seen. She busied
herself arranging flowers at the dining room table and placed
a stuffed penguin by Caroline Lane's place setting. When she
was finished preparing the table Lionel inspected her work.
As he adjusted the water glasses, he said, 'Water glasses
always three inches northeast of the wine goblets.'

'Yes sir. Sorry.'

Again he gazed at her searchingly. 'Are you sure you're feeling all right? You seem nervous, preoccupied.'

'I didn't sleep well,' she said. 'But I'll be fine.'

As they crossed to the entry hall the door buzzer sounded
and Rufus let out a deep and powerful series of barks.

'I'll get it,' Marshall called out from the bedroom. 'C'mon,
Rufus, let's go greet the lady.'

But it was Neta, the dog sitter, with three dogs on a leash.
She petted Rufus, whose tail was waving wildly in anticipa-
tion of the out of doors. She said to Marshall, 'How long do
you want me to keep him out for?'

'I'd say an hour, but – no, make it two hours.' He smiled. 'I
may be detained a bit longer than planned.'

Marisa, standing discreetly in the foyer, shot a quick look
at him. Tan trousers, an open blue shirt, a tweed jacket. He
looked so handsome and so happy. And very excited. If only I
could be anywhere but here, she thought. My God . . . what if
he recognizes me? She couldn't bear to carry the thought to
its logical conclusion.

Just as Neta was leaving with her brood, Caroline Lane
swept into the open door, practically bowling her over. She
was dressed in the carefully chosen skirt and blouse, and
Marisa had to admit that she looked striking. When one of

the dogs, an apricot miniature poodle, sniffed at her crotch she jumped away quickly. 'No, no,' she said nervously.

She gave Chris Marshall her most dazzling smile.

'You're an animal lover too?' she said, her accent, Marisa thought, slightly more upper class than usual.

Marshall stared at her, his expression one of total confusion. 'Sorry?'

'I can't get enough of them,' she gushed. The poodle persisted in sniffing at her. She backed away, shaking a finger at the dog. 'Naughty, naughty,' she cried. She turned back to Marshall, her eyes bright. 'What a simply divine idea. Lunch *à deux*. So lovely!'

Neta and the dogs left, the door slamming behind them.

Marshall continued to stare at her as though looking for something – someone – that wasn't there. 'Caroline?' He started to say more, but she stopped him by offering up her cheek for a kiss; he leaned forward and reluctantly gave her a quick peck, then quickly backed off.

With a show of sinuous grace Caroline moved into the dining room. 'I just knew we made a connection at the Feathered Friends tournament in Southampton, and oh, *look*' – she picked up the stuffed penguin – 'how very sweet of you to remember.'

Marshall could not stop staring at her. He seemed to be willing her to morph into the woman he had expected to see walk in the door. He had no idea what to say, how to act. Most important was the question burning in his mind: *Who the hell are you?*

'But I hope you didn't think I needed reminding,' she rambled on. 'Please don't think me forward for telling you this – but I sensed something special last summer. A frisson. . . .'

Marshall shot Lionel a helpless look, which the head butler returned impassively.

Caroline touched Marshall's sleeve. 'By the way, Teddy Parrish sends his best.'

At least he knew Teddy Parrish, though he'd rather that he didn't. The stupid ass had been his classmate at Princeton. 'Ted. Oh yes. How is he?'

'Drinking again. But you didn't hear that from me. Dear Teddy is very, very weak, I'm afraid.' She wandered back into the living room and plunked herself down on the couch, still smiling radiantly.

'Excuse me a minute,' he said. 'I have to check on something.'

Marisa turned away as he approached Lionel in the dining room.

'Who is that woman?' he said in a whisper, nodding his head in her direction. She was craning her neck to read something on the end table. She swiveled over to the edge of the couch, picked up the invitation to the Maddox event on Monday, quickly read it and put it back.

Snoop, thought Marisa, who had been watching her out of the corner of her eye. The woman's all manner and all bad manners. She must've never got a good spanking.

'I don't know her,' Marshall said. 'Or if I do, it's a slight acquaintance. The point is, she's not the woman I invited here. Who is she?'

'Caroline Lane, sir.'

'No.' Marshall shook his head emphatically. 'That is not Caroline Lane.'

Lionel cleared his throat. 'I'm afraid it is, sir.'

'Chris?' Caroline called, giving his name three lilting sylla-

120

bles. 'I loved your quote in the *Times*.' She patted the couch and scooted over. 'Come sit with me.'

He sat, leaving a foot of space between them.

'You know,' he said nonchalantly, 'it's really very strange.'

'What's strange, my dear?' She squiggled inches closer to him.

'There's someone,' he said. 'I can't figure out where I've seen her before.'

'What do you mean. Someone I know?'

'Yes. The woman visiting you the other day. Kind of, ah, Latino or Mediterranean, with a little boy about ten. . . .'

Lionel stopped what he was doing and stared at Marshall, then slowly he turned his implacable visage on Marisa, who was busily polishing silver.

Caroline looked puzzled. 'Rachel Hoffberg? Latino or Mediterranean? I don't think so. She's a nice Jewish girl from Westport, and she's pre-menopausal, but don't tell her I said so.'

'Huh?' Marshall took a deep breath, trying to hide his growing annoyance with this woman and her silly, random chatter. What was she doing here? How had she ended up here? And how could he get her to go away? After a pause that was beginning to grow awkward, he said, 'You're in the Park Suite, right?'

'Yes.' She smiled cute. 'As you well know.'

Marshall shrugged. 'It's the damnedest thing. Oh well.'

In the York Suite kitchenette an apprehensive Marisa was folding a linen towel and neatly wrapping the neck of a bottle of white burgundy chilling in a silver ice bucket. Lionel was supervising her, watching her with special attention. He started to say something to her, but then tightened his lips.

121

They could hear the murmur of voices from the living room and could catch an occasional word. Caroline was doing most of the talking.

'Tuck the towel in tight,' Lionel said, breaking the silence.

Suddenly Marshall bolted through the louvered doors. He looked distraught and his hair stood up in back where he had kept nervously running his hand through it.

'Lionel,' he said in a whisper, a note of desperation in his voice.

Marisa froze, her back to him.

'Sir?'

'The woman I'm talking about – she's about five feet six, dark haired, extremely pretty – I'd call her beautiful – and she has a kid named Ty. I didn't dream all this. What the hell happened? Where is she? I think I'm going nuts.'

Lionel shot a sidelong glance at Marisa, then said, 'I'm sorry, sir.'

'Don't be sorry. Just find her for me.'

He reluctantly returned to the living room. Caroline patted the cushion beside her and he sat down.

'I just love your speeches,' she said. 'I follow them.'

'You . . . follow them?'

She laughed soft chimes and said, 'Silly me – I mean I *read* them. And did I tell you? I loved your quote in the *Times*.'

'You told me.'

'Politics must be very exciting.'

'Not really. It's basically a selling job. Selling your ideas and selling yourself. Not exactly glamorous.'

'My crystal ball tells me you have a gorgeous career ahead of you.'

He held up a hand. 'Please,' he pleaded.

Finally they were called to lunch.

'Everything looks absolutely scrumptious,' she observed gaily.

Marshall nodded as he stared gloomily at the wine Lionel was pouring.

'We're all here to try to land the Buchwald estate,' Caroline confided. 'Christie's thought they'd locked it up, but I'm meeting the great aunt tomorrow morning. The jewelry alone is worth half a billion.'

'Really?' Marshall said, barely listening. Boredom had set in like sticky glue, clogging his senses.

'But I want to hear more about you.'

'There's not very much to say. My life is pretty much drudge work.'

'Not according to the papers,' she said with a little laugh.

As Marisa brought a dish to the sideboard, Caroline turned and saw her.

'Oh Maria,' she said.

Marisa's back was to the table, but she could feel his eyes on her. She couldn't breathe. 'Miss?' she said, deliberately lowering her voice.

'Could I get a couple of ice cubes?'

Marisa, saying a silent prayer (*God, please God, help me through this mess!*), started to turn around, but Lionel stepped in. Taking a bowl and a spoon from the serving cart, he inserted himself between Marisa and the table with a couple of quick strides.

'Allow me,' he said.

He spooned some ice into the glass, his expression unreadable. He turned away without a glance and said, 'That will be all, Miss Ventura.'

She left the room, forcing herself not to hurry.

Later in the afternoon Marisa changed into her street clothes in the locker room and tied the belt of her light raincoat. The weather had changed and was promising rain. She pulled a red rain hat over her hair and handed Ty a windbreaker she kept in her locker for emergencies.

'Put this on,' she said. 'I don't want you to get your clothes wet for the party.'

'It's not raining out.'

'It's supposed to. Let's not take a chance.'

Ty looked at the photograph of the employee of the month and read the writing on the plaque beneath it.

'Hey, Ma,' he said. 'What's it mean – "strain to be invisible"? Isn't that kind of weird?'

She zipped up his windbreaker. 'I don't know, Ty. Come on. We got a lot to do.'

They walked quickly through the basement area.

'Is that a good thing?'

'What?'

'Invisibility.'

'Oh – they don't mean that literally. It's just that people like to have things done for them, and they don't want to see who's doing it.'

'That sounds kind of strange.'

'Well, it's the way things are.'

'The way things are,' he repeated thoughtfully. 'Well, I don't ever want you to be invisible for me, OK?'

She squeezed his hand. 'Yeah, honey, OK.' She kept his hand in hers as they continued walking.

At the security desk Keef's monitors were tracking the

coming and going of people on the different floors. He looked up as Marisa and Ty walked by.

Marisa nodded and gave the older man a wink and a grin. 'We're just running over to Barnes & Noble for a few minutes.'

Keef's features were wreathed in a slow smile. 'Another interestin' day, huh, Marisa?'

'I don't know. Was it?'

'You tell me.' His grin grew wider. 'Nice lunch on the twenty-second floor?'

Marisa gave him a one-eyed squint. ' 'Sup, mystery man? You got somethin' to tell me?'

'Well,' he drawled, 'how many times you watched the monitors with me? How many times we enjoyed the comin's and goin's of the high and mighty?'

'Thousands,' Ty put in with a mischievous look at his mother.

'And what did we see today, young man?'

'Oh – some comin's and goin's.'

Marisa glared at them both. 'Ty – wait over there. I want to speak to Keef alone.'

'But, Ma, he's just—'

'Ty! Over there.'

He walked a few feet away but strained to hear her as she leaned close to Keef. 'So what gives, God?'

'Well, you know, Marisa,' Keef said in his lazy, melodious drawl, 'I'm obliged to report employees misbehaving.'

Marisa stared at him, not knowing whether to laugh or to frown. To her knowledge, Keef had never reported a single wrong doing to management in all his years on the job.

'There's only one thing could make me shut my mouth.'

'And what could that one thing be, Keef?'

He looked her straight in the eye, then closed his, leaned forward and puckered his lips. She smiled in spite of herself and could hear Ty giggling.

'Why you dirty old man.'

'Never was too young to be that.' He gave Ty a thumbs-up gesture. 'We had a good day at the monitors, didn't we, boy?'

'A very good day, Keef.'

Marisa took Ty's hand. 'You're in trouble, young man. You're both in trouble.'

As they were leaving Keef called after her, 'You save me a dance at the party, now. For hush money, you know.'

11

At the very moment Marisa and Ty were leaving the Beresford to shop at Barnes & Noble, the two French poodles, Monique and Anouk, were in the hotel lobby preparing to check out. John Bextrum and a night maid approached them and their mountain of luggage. 'I hope you ladies had a good stay with us,' Bextrum said.

'Excellent,' Monique said.

'A lovely hotel,' Anouk added.

His eyes darting around to see if they were being watched, Bextrum reached into a shopping bag and removed three terry cloth robes.

'Unfortunately, ladies, the robes are not complimentary.'

'Fine,' Monique said haughtily. 'This is not a problem.'

'We would be happy to add them to your account. . . .'

'We took them for a greater purpose,' Anouk said. 'We were going to give them to the homeless.'

Bextrum trained his polite smile on her, not quite as polished as usual, however, and showing a little strain. 'How interesting. Robes to the homeless.'

The night maid whispered something to Bextrum.

'Ah, yes,' he said, nodding. 'Ladies, there's also the matter of the silver soap dishes. And, I understand, some pieces of silverware. . . .'

Maintaining her hauteur, and knowing they were caught dead to rights, Monique said, 'Charge our account, Mr Bextrum, if you would be so kind. We have a plane to catch.'

'I will do that, Madame,' he said gravely, with a slight bow, shifting his glance to Caroline Lane and a friend who swept by on their way to the concierge desk.

'I'm Caroline Lane,' she said in a carrying voice, 'in the Park Suite.'

'Yes, Madame?'

'I called about getting a ticket to the Maddox benefit tomorrow night.'

'Yes,' he said. 'We were able to procure you a single at a table on the main floor, adjacent to Mr Marshall's.'

'Not at his table?'

'I'm afraid that wasn't possible, Madame.'

She sighed and sucked her teeth. 'How much?' she snapped.

'Three thousand dollars,' the concierge answered. 'The rates are raised when a couple is split. Singles are always harder to place.'

Caroline leaned across the counter and hissed, 'What is it, on the internet? *I'm an ex-couple?*'

'Madame, you understand I'm talking about tickets, not—'

'Does the whole hotel know?' she said, too angry to hear

him. 'Is there a Biblical sign on my forehead – unclean? *Unmarried*? Do I bear the scarlet letter?'

'Caroline, for God's sake,' Rachel put in.

'I'm talking about single tickets,' the concierge said, looking Bextrum's way with concern.

'What?'

'It's the tickets, dear, not you,' Rachel said. Lowering her voice, she said, 'Get a grip.'

'I know, *I know*,' Caroline said. She turned back to the concierge and managed a smile. 'Charge it to my room, please.'

'Certainly, Madame.' He nodded warily, not meeting her agitated gaze.

Just as Caroline and Rachel exited the Beresford, Marshall and Jerry Seigal were passing the hotel in a town car.

'My God, it's her!' Marshall exclaimed, sliding down low in his seat, his head below window level.

'Who?'

'That woman. The monster who came to lunch. Did she spot us?'

'All clear.'

Marshall let out a long sigh. 'How did this happen – this – this French farce? There has to be an explanation.'

'I think she's very attractive.'

'But she's not the woman I wanted. She's not the woman I invited to lunch. And I don't find her the least bit attractive. A society phony through and through. I've known dozens like her.'

'I don't know what to tell you, buddy. I really don't. I spoke to the manager and he assured me she's the only Caroline Lane staying in the Park Suite – in fact the only Caroline

Lane in the hotel, period.'

As the town car crawled through the late-afternoon Sunday traffic, Marshall stared gloomily out the window. Suddenly he sat up straight and, pointing, he said, 'That's them! Ty and Caroline!' They turned a corner and walked west toward Madison Avenue.

'Pull over, driver.'

Before the car came to a full stop at the curb, Marshall had the door open and was jumping out. 'Hey,' he yelled, 'wait up!'

'Hey Chris. . . .' Ty gave him a wide grin and a high five. Marisa stared at him, looking stunned.

'Do you want to hear something really strange?' he said, giving Marisa a probing look. 'I invited you to lunch today and you came, only it wasn't you. What happened?'

'I don't know what you mean.'

'But that butler, Lionel, he assured me you got the invitation. And somebody who called herself Caroline Lane came to lunch, but she definitely was not the one I invited. I invited *you*.'

'I'm afraid I can't solve your mystery.'

'Are you still staying at the Beresford?'

'No – actually we moved uptown. Way uptown.'

'Great,' he said. 'Hop in. I'll give you a ride wherever you're going. We're on our way to Harlem. So we'll drop you where – upper Eastside?'

'Ah, no thanks. We've got this party a few blocks from here and right now we're on our way to Barnes & Noble.'

'How do I get in touch with you?'

She tried to avoid his eyes with their power to pull her in and leave her without defenses. He was trouble. She wanted him to go away and stay out of her life. But another part of her was thrilled that he had materialized at the very moment she was thinking of him.

Ty said, 'Her cell is nine-one-seven—'

Marisa interrupted, saying, 'How 'bout I call you?'

Jerry Seigal rushed up and handed her a card. 'You can reach Mr Marshall through me. What's your last name?'

'Lane,' Ty said, answering for her. 'What's yours?'

'Seigal.' He checked his watch. 'Chris, we've got to run. We don't want to be late for this.'

Marshall reached for Marisa's hand and she felt the heat of his intense glance. 'Use that number, Caroline. Please.'

She put Seigal's card in her pocket and smiled.

'Listen,' Seigal said, 'you very much need to give a speech you're about to be late for. I don't think that's a great idea.'

'In Harlem?' Marisa said. 'On what?'

'Housing projects,' Marshall answered. 'How to get the neighborhoods working again.'

'Really?' She gave a short laugh, on the border between skeptical and derisive. 'You're talking to people in Harlem about the projects, the people who live in them day in, day out? That's . . . interesting.'

'We think so,' Seigal said impatiently. 'Chris – come on, man. We've got to move it.'

Marshall started to get in the car but then he hesitated and turned to Marisa. 'What are you *not* saying, Caroline?'

She took a deep breath. 'Nothing.'

'Tell me,' he said. 'I want to know what you're thinking. I really want to know.'

'Tell him, Ma,' Ty said.

'Well,' she began haltingly, 'what I think is, I think maybe the two of you should spend some real time in the projects. Not just a quick in and out. Get to know the people, talk to them, get a taste of what life is like up there. You should stay a while, not just give a speech but hear what others have to say. Then you won't need any speeches to memorize. It'll come from somewhere else – some honest place.'

Marshall shook his head, his blue eyes burning into her. 'That's pretty eloquent,' he said. 'And the truth is, I don't have the slightest idea how to respond.' He smiled. 'When you render a politician speechless, you've really accomplished something.'

'I still hear you talking,' she said, returning his smile.

'Just spinning wheels, believe me.'

Seigal suddenly went on the attack. 'What makes you an authority anyway, Ms Lane?'

'Well, I grew up there,' Marisa answered. 'I lived in a four-block world my whole life. I doubt there's much either of you could tell me that I don't know or offer advice I haven't heard a thousand times from well-meaning folks like you. . . .' Her eyes swept over Marshall briefly. 'Good night.'

She and Ty continued walking toward Madison Avenue.

The town car drove off, and for a moment Seigal and Marshall sat in silence, Marshall slumped down in his seat, eyes closed.

'Who the hell is that woman?' Seigal said finally.

'I'll tell you who she isn't. She isn't like anyone I've ever known before. She isn't a phony. She isn't full of a lot of theories and pseudo educated hot air. She doesn't talk down to

132

people. I know one thing about her, Jerry – she's the real deal.'

'Come on, you can't possibly know that. I sense a little ghetto there, to be honest with you.'

'You're wrong.' Marshall sat up straight and turned to his chief of staff. 'I have an assignment for you,' he said.

'Shoot, boss.'

'Well, it's more like a deal. A deal you can't refuse.'

'So? You got my attention.'

'You want me at this benefit tomorrow night? Well, then you have to get her to accept my invitation.'

'*Her?*'

'Her. And if you can pull that off, Kemo Sabe, I swear to God I'll shake any part of Maddox's body you want me to. Do we have a deal?'

Seigal thought about it, muttering to himself. 'You drive a hard bargain.'

'Yes or no?'

He sighed and stuck out his hand. 'You got it,' he said.

By six o'clock the Beresford party in honor of the departing assistant manager Christina Howard was in full swing in the cafeteria. Loud, pulsing music with a pronounced disco beat filled the room. Even off hours the caste system was still in effect: maids with maids, valets with valets, butlers with butlers, kitchen staff with kitchen staff, maintenance men in coveralls gathered around a table drinking beer and shooting dice for dollars. Non-dancers stood against the wall observing the action while room service waiters danced with maids. The butlers, like the valets, were more watchers than participants and seemed to be having less fun than the others, as though their relatively exalted position in the Beresford social strata was weighing heavily on them. Only management moved freely among the various groups, dishing out cheery noblesse oblige.

Ty spent the next three hours handing CDs to the DJ, Mugsy Gorshin. By nine o'clock the dance floor was filled; Mugsy put on 'Good Times' and the dancing took on greater intensity.

Marisa and Stephanie watched from a table nearby. 'Great tune,' Marisa said, moving to the music. 'Makes you want to jiggle.'

'You've done a whole lot of jiggling tonight. Not like you, girl.

'I know. I'm in a manic mood.'

Stephanie shouted to the DJ, 'Hey Mugs, keep playing stuff like that, Marisa and I are gonna have to pull out some new moves.'

'So pull 'em, ladies,' he shouted back. 'I'd love to see Marisa really get down.'

'You may live to regret that,' Marisa said, laughing.

'You been sittin' out long enough, girls,' Mugsy said. 'Let's get those backfields in motion now.'

'Hey, Maris,' Stephanie said, nudging her. 'Four o'clock, by the lasagna tray. Check *that* out.' A large muscular man with a mustache stood, swaying slightly to the beat.

'Some hunk, huh? I mean truly studly.'

'Hum,' Marisa said, giving him a glance. 'Working class Valentino.'

'So?'

'Not my type.'

'He's Tito from shipping. Only been here a couple days.

I've already scoped him out.'

'Slut,' Marisa said, laughing.

'I'd rather call myself a randy girl with healthy appetites.'

'Steph,' Marisa said, lowering her voice, 'seven o'clock by the bulletin board.' Lionel stood by the entrance, observing the crowd.

'The great Lionel Bloch,' Stephanie said. 'So what? I see enough of him during the daytime.'

'I wonder why he just arrived. I'm worried about him.'

'Why?'

'I like him.'

'Well, I don't. He's a prick. No heart, no soul.'

'I think he hides a lot of himself,' Marisa said. 'Also I don't think he's well.'

'He drinks like a fish.'

'That's just scuttlebutt.'

'You kidding? I've smelled it on his breath.'

'I haven't seen him since lunch,' Marisa said. 'That's unusual. Something's up.'

'Give me a break. Why are you all concerned about an old fart who wouldn't give you the time of day? You think he gives a rat's ass about you and your problems? I can tell you this – Bextrum's on him like shit on shit.'

'Oh yeah? Why?'

'Old Lionel's got the shakes. It seems to be plain to everybody but you that the man's a lush. Rumor is he's gonna be let go if he doesn't straighten up.' She mimed taking a drink from a bottle.

Marisa shook her head. 'I don't believe it, Steph. A lot of people have it in for him because . . . well, he's a very private person. He has a lot of pride, and he's not all palsy-walsy with

135

management. I know he's sick. I can tell.'

'You shoulda been a nun. You're all charity and mercy.'

'Well I can't help it – I like him. Besides, he helped me out this afternoon. He didn't have to.'

Stephanie inclined her head toward Bextrum who was making his rounds. 'Grow up, girl. Lionel's one of them. Management. Don't kid yourself. He'd sacrifice you in a New York second.' She took a sip of her punch and rose. 'Now I'm gonna go and be neighborly. And I think I'll start with Tito who looks a little lonely. I suggest you do the same.' She sucked in her tummy, straightened her dress and walked over to the muscular shipping clerk, passing Lionel who had advanced into the room as far as the punch bowl. Bextrum strolled up and extended his hand to the head butler. The moment was awkward as Lionel's hands shook at his side.

'Mr Bextrum,' said Marisa, who suddenly appeared at his side, diverting his attention from Lionel. She put a cup of punch in his hand. 'Here you go,' she said with a smile.

'Why thank you, Miss Ventura.' He looked surprised and pleased, and he bestowed his most polished smile on her. Then he turned back to Lionel and his smile faded. 'We'll talk tomorrow, Lionel.'

'Very good,' the butler said stoically.

As Bextrum moved on to mix with the crowd, Marisa ladled out a cup of punch for Lionel.

'Are you OK?' she said.

'I'm fine,' he said icily as he accepted the cup. 'Thank you.'

'I just want to explain about this afternoon,' she said awkwardly. 'I mean I realize it must have looked unusual . . . maybe inappropriate . . . but. . . .'

'I don't know what you're referring to,' Lionel cut in, 'and

I prefer to keep it that way.' He set his punch on the table untouched and slowly walked around the perimeter of the improvised dance floor. A large crowd was now dancing to the somewhat softer beat of Stevie Wonder. Marisa watched as he put on his bowler and slowly left the party.

12

The next morning at the Beresford started as usual with the staff gathered for their morning briefing with Paula Burns, but shortly after it started Marisa saw something that began the progress of tilting her world off its axis. Jerry Seigal was standing in the doorway, his head swinging back and forth searching for something or someone.

'Jesus,' Marisa breathed to Stephanie, 'hide me.'

She slipped behind her friend and the ample form of Clarice.

'You playin' hide-n-seek, girl?' Clarice said. 'Or is that geek in the doorway one of them stalkers. He sure do look like one.'

'Sh,' Marisa said.

'Heads up, people,' Paula Burns called out. 'The Shapiros have requested early check in, so we'll put them in the Dior Suite. . . .'

Stephanie whispered, 'It's OK. He's ducked back out.'

'Oh God, he's back,' Marisa said a moment later, peeking at the door from the space between Stephanie and Clarice. Seigal had reappeared and he was in deep conversation with Lionel.

'Uh oh,' Stephanie said.

'I have a feeling my goose is cooked.'

'Well, you better eat it then 'fore it spoils,' Clarice said.

Seigal continued to talk and Lionel was nodding. Then Seigal left and Lionel headed back to the meeting.

Paula Burns was saying, 'Mr Newman and his mother will keep the Hudson Suite till four o'clock. . . .'

Lionel caught Marisa's eye and motioned for her to join him. A moment later, his mouth compressed in a tight line, he punched the elevator button for the Beresford roof, the last level directly above the penthouse floor. There was no one on the floor except for a single bell man smoking on the other end, well away from them.

'Is there something wrong, Mr Bloch?'

He stared at her for a moment before handing her an embossed envelope.

'There is nothing wrong with you, Miss Ventura. With the world, yes, most definitely.'

She fingered the invitation. 'What is this?'

'I think you know.'

She nodded. 'I think I know, too.'

'It seems that my job is at risk unless you appear at this evening's benefit.'

'Mr Seigal is putting pressure on you? That's terrible.'

'I might not be the only one he put pressure on.'

Marisa's hand flew to her mouth. 'Oh my God. You mean others may know.'

Lionel nodded. 'My point exactly. Right now he has no idea who you are. It's a mystery he has been asked to solve. But how long do you think it will take him to discover that the woman with the son named Ty was cleaning the Park Suite, not staying there? Put quite simply, Miss Ventura, I don't see that you have any choice. I suggest that we accept this invitation immediately.'

'Are you going too?' she said hopefully.

A hint of a smile appeared on his lips. 'I meant the royal "we".'

'Oh,' she said, not understanding. She reached out and touched Lionel's sleeve. He continued to look at her unblinkingly as though he hadn't been touched. 'I can't believe Mr Marshall would put him up to this. He doesn't seem like that kind of man.'

'I'm fairly certain he had nothing to do with it.' Lionel hesitated. 'His chief of staff has his own way of doing things.'

'He's ruthless.'

'This is not the time for recriminations,' Lionel said. 'The question is, do you agree to this arrangement. It's entirely up to you.'

'Do I have any choice?'

'I suppose you do. But then you and I will both be gone.'

'That's no choice.'

'I suppose not.'

'I'm going,' she said. 'That's settled. I'll go.'

Lionel studied her as though he were examining a place setting to make certain that forks and knives, plates and glasses were in their proper place. 'We'll make sure you have the proper costume and accoutrements,' he said.

She nodded, overwhelmed.

'And another thing,' he continued. 'After tonight you're to make sure that you never see him again. Do I make myself clear?'

'Mr Seigal's order, right?'

'It doesn't matter. Is it clear, Miss Ventura?'

'Perfectly,' said Stephanie, walking up to them, a lighted cigarette hanging from her lip. 'I would say "what a coincidence" finding you two here on the roof. But I had a feeling you were looking for a little privacy.'

'And you were quite right, Miss Kehoe,' Lionel said drily.

She regarded him with a smile. 'You know, Lionel, and you don't mind me calling you Lionel, right? You know, you're really a pretty cool dude to help out this way. A lot of people think you're a stuck-up snob.'

'Steph!' Marisa said, glancing apprehensively at Lionel.

But he seemed more amused than angry. 'I should point out that I'm hardly a disinterested party, Miss Kehoe. My job is at stake.'

'Whatever you say, I still think you're cool. You're going to bat for my friend.'

'How kind. I assume you know what's going on.'

'You assume right. It wasn't hard to put two and two together. I know about the affair tonight and I saw that creep hassling you.'

Lionel slowly tore his eyes from Stephanie and trained them on Marisa. 'Now I've taken care of your schedule for the rest of the day.'

'She's gonna need some immoral support,' Stephanie pointed out.

'I think you mean moral.'

'That's the sweetest thing you've ever said to me, sir,' she said with a big grin.

'I guess I can arrange your schedule too, Miss Kehoe.'

'Fantastic! We'll be like a couple of stealth bombshells. You won't even know we're here but we'll get it done'

Again he seemed about to smile. 'I'll cling to that notion,' he said.

Anyone who works in a large hotel for any length of time is bound to develop a large network of friends and partners in crime, and that was true of Marisa and Stephanie. They knew the people who made the Beresford hum, unsung people perhaps but vital to. the hotel's successful functioning – the florists, the tailors, the manicurists, hairdressers, sales girls – and the two friends swam through the hotel's bloodstream, passing the word, uniting their friends, these working women, behind them. Magic had to be performed today and in a matter of hours.

Frances was waiting for them at the entrance to the Valentino store in the lobby. 'Here they are, Michelle!' she called out to the sales girl in the back. She grabbed Marisa in a huge embrace. 'Hi there, Cinderella, this is gonna be a night to remember.' She ushered Stephanie and Marisa into the back room where Michelle was waiting with dozens of Valentino originals all lined up for Marisa's inspection. Lily was there with pins and thread.

'We've only got an hour before Myrna comes in on her broom. C'mon, girls, let's shake and bake!'

Marisa twirled around in the backroom in one gorgeous dress after another, putting on a veritable fashion show.

'I want to wear them all,' she exclaimed.

Stephanie laughed. 'Of course you do, honey. What woman wouldn't?'

Ty and Keef, in the meantime, stood at the counter of Harry

Winston's jewelry store in the Beresford lobby. Cora, the saleswoman, smiled nervously as she said, 'OK, Ty, let's run through this drill one more time.'

He smiled pleasantly. 'OK.'

'Focus now. Eyes forward.'

'The boy is always focused,' Keef said. 'Don't worry about him.'

Ty stood straight, intent on her words.

'Once more,' she said. 'This is the Harry Winston Wreath necklace.'

Ty nodded. 'I know. Worth more than I'll earn in ten life-times.'

'Good. What else?'

'If it leaves my mother's neck at any time, I'll be put up for adoption while she rots in prison. Your exact words.'

'Good boy! And I should add that I'll be right there in the cell with her.'

She started to hand him the suitcase, but Keef reached for it.

'I'm guarding him,' he said. 'I made Marisa a promise.'

Cora said sarcastically, 'This makes me feel so much better.'

'Why Cora, dear. Don't you trust me?'

'You scalawag, anything happens there's a cell waiting for you too.'

'Put your fears to rest.'

Cora reached across the counter and pinched Ty's cheek. 'Bye, honey. And wish your mom all kinds of luck.'

In the hotel spa, Elle, the manicurist, was working on Marisa's nails when Ty and Keef brought her the jewelry. She opened the suitcase and stared at the necklace, open-mouthed. 'My

God,' she said. I've never seen anything so beautiful. . . .'

'Keep 'em on your neck at all times,' Keef said, 'else it's jail time for all of us.'

'Where are the earrings?' Stephanie said.

Ty dug in his pocket and produced them. Marisa held them in her hand and smiled, a faraway look in her eyes. 'If I'm dreaming, people, please don't wake me up.'

Keef handed her another box and, bowing deeply, said, 'Your Manolo–Blahnik shoes, Madame,' doing his down-South imitation of Lionel Bloch.

'Don't scuff 'em, Ma,' Ty said. 'More jail time.'

Shortly after five o'clock that afternoon the seamstress shop was filled with people. Since the stores in the lobby had just closed, Michelle, Frances, Elle and Cora were standing expectantly by the little curtained-off changing room, along with Ty, Keef, Stephanie, Clarice and Barbara. They were waiting for the unveiling.

They could hear Lily's voice inside the changing room. 'OK, hold still, Marisa. Here. Let me just pin this. Good. Let me look at you. . . .' A moment of silence while all of those waiting held a collective breath.

'*Voilà!*' Lily cried, opening the curtain. Marisa stepped out smiling and did a slow turn for her audience.

Ty's jaw dropped.

Stephanie snapped a series of pictures.

Barbara whistled.

Keef said, 'Wow!'

Clarice said, 'My God, girl, you're a queen!'

And then the group broke out in applause.

Marisa curtsied.

*

Two hours later, Ty leaned in the open window of the limousine idling at the Beresford service entrance and planted a kiss on his mother's cheek. Stephanie stood beside him, smiling, her eyes moist.

'Bye, Ma,' Ty said. 'Have fun.'

'Thanks, sweetie. Listen to Stephanie now – and go to bed when she tells you – OK? No negotiating.'

'Break a leg,' he said.

'What?'

'That's a show business term. It means give a great performance – wow the audience.'

'I know.'

Stephanie leaned in the window, touched her fingers to her lips and blew Marisa a kiss.

'Oh God, I can't breathe,' Marisa said. 'What am I doing here, Steph? This is crazy. It's all a lie.'

'No, honey,' Stephanie said quietly. 'It's more like a dream, you know? And for one night you're living it for all of us. Don't think about tomorrow, don't think about anything but tonight. Tonight the maid is a lie – and this, *this*, is who you really are . . . a true princess.'

Marisa fought back tears as she squeezed her friend's hand.

'I don't know what I'm doing,' she said in wonder. 'For the first time in my life I don't seem to be in control.'

'And how does it feel?'

'Not so bad,' Marisa said. 'In fact it feels kind of wonderful.'

13

The Metropolitan Museum of Art reception area was beginning to fill with black cocktail dresses, tuxedos and well-known faces as the gala got underway. The noise was already deafening and Chris Marshall, his party smile fixed firmly in place, felt besieged. People were descending on him like so many mosquitoes in a hot swamp, wishing him well and wanting to warm themselves in his aura, if only for a moment.

A burly hand clapped down hard on his shoulder. He turned to Harry Schiff, a TV producer with a big heart and an even bigger mouth. He was a recent apostate in the liberal show business community, having abandoned them to switch allegiance to Marshall in his run for his father's senate seat. Publicly mocked by some of his liberal friends – although many others joined him in favoring Marshall over his opponent whom many considered an old Democratic party hack – Schiff responded with an op-ed piece in the *New York Post* in which he made his case for Christopher Marshall. 'I don't consider Christopher Marshall a

Democrat *or* a Republican,' he wrote. 'The labels are fast losing their distinction. I consider him a man who unerringly makes good choices, which benefit people, not corporations. . . .'

Grabbing Marshall's arm in a firm grip, he said, 'What do you need, Chris? Tell me what you need.'

Marshall returned his arm squeeze. 'Just your support, Harry. That means a lot.'

'What about a cameo on *Saturday Night Live*?'

'Ah, let's wait on that. I'm not sure I want Darrel Hammond imitating me. Look where it got Gore.'

'I'm calling Lorne. You'd be a natural and that kind of exposure translates into votes.'

Seigal swooped in on the conversation, saying, 'Harry, good to see you.'

'Jerry, I was just telling your candidate he should be on SNL. I can arrange it with Lorne.'

'Terrific, fantastic, Harry. We'll talk tomorrow.'

Seigal and Marshall left Schiff behind and navigated the school of well-wishers swimming frantically in the celebrity sea.

'You spent too much time with Harry Schiff,' Seigal whispered in Marshall's ear. 'He's already in our pocket. Use your time, man.'

A moment later Seigal said enthusiastically, 'Chris – look who's here!' A well known, much-divorced socialite, Denise Gordon, very rich and a potential Marshall supporter, stepped up and offered him her cheek.

'Denise,' Marshall said, dutifully kissing her cheek. 'Great seeing you.'

'And you, darling.' She pressed in closer and said, 'Your

speech at the Nature Conservancy. Shivers! Simply shivers!'

'Thank you.'

'We must get together. Lunch, dinner. I was a great admirer of your father.'

'I know. And I appreciate that.'

The smile Marshall was working started to crack, and Seigal broke in, saying, 'Denise, wonderful to see you again. Binky Osmond was just asking for you.' He called out, 'Binky?' He turned Denise Gordon around and pointed her in the direction of the main ballroom. 'Wonderful to see you looking so well,' he said, sending her on her way.

He took Marshall's arm and guided him through the crowd. 'Sixty if she's a day. She wants your bod, kid.'

'That's revolting.'

'There's big, big bucks there. It won't hurt to make her feel young and beautiful.'

'I need you to protect me from women like that, Jerry, or I'll have your head.'

'A heavy contributor, if we land her.'

'Life is too short.'

'Says you.' Seigal pointed toward the entrance. 'Maddox just arrived with Congressman Grey. Your job is to butter up the old man.'

Seigal waved to the congressman and Maddox.

'C'mon, Chris, let's show a little enthusiasm here.'

Marshall's eyes were scanning the room.

'*What*?' Seigal said impatiently.

'Is she here?'

'Not yet. She will be. C'mon, man, we've got work to do.'

The formal benefit was now in full swing. In a swaying sea of tuxedos and little black dresses floated the usual exotic specimens that attend these affairs – real estate magnates, corporate moguls, *60 Minutes* correspondents, Norman Mailer, the Baldwin brothers (recent converts to Marshall's cause), the Hilton sisters, Tim Robbins and Susan Sarandon (also recent converts), and a pack of wannabees clawing their way up the Manhattan social ladder an expensive rung at a time.

Marshall and Congressman Grey chatted animatedly as they walked through the ballroom.

'You remind me so much of your father,' the older man said.

'Thank you, sir. I consider that a compliment.'

'A bit more to the left of center, however,' he said, clearing his throat.

'I see it as a gradual evolution rather than an actual change in philosophies,' Marshall said smoothly. 'My father and I saw the world through similar eyes.'

As they continued to talk, a number of people, including Seigal and Maddox tagging along in their wake, watched the power dance: the younger politician paying court to the older statesman.

'Chris Marshall comports himself well,' Maddox observed.

'He should,' Seigal replied, laughing. 'He's been trained by yours truly.' He held up a hand. 'Just joking.'

Suddenly Marshall stopped short. He saw Marisa at the entrance and drew in a quick breath. He couldn't stop staring at her she looked so breathtaking. Many other eyes were on her, too, especially women's eyes, trying to place her in a context they could understand. Who was this gorgeous young woman? The noise surrounding her had dropped a decibel.

As Marshall watched her, she smiled and crossed the bridge that had been built over a 'moat' into the party.

'Excuse me, Congressman,' Marshall said. 'Perhaps we can talk later?'

'Of course.'

Marshall and Marisa moved toward each other, their eyes fastened on each other. Many in the room were aware of the two of them, sensing their magnetism, including Caroline Lane who coldly appraised the radiant presence that had created a subtle but sudden impact on the gathering. She sized the stranger up with a growing sense that she looked familiar.

Marshall took Marisa's hand and guided her to the dance floor.

'You're some knockout,' he said.

'So are you, Mr Assemblyman.'

She looked around self-consciously, aware of all the eyes on her.

'Thank you for being here,' he said.

'You don't need to thank me. I'm thrilled out of my mind.'

'I'm very glad to hear that.'

'But I need to tell you . . . tell you now . . . that this – you and me – it's not going to happen again. Not beyond this evening. It can't.'

'Then you should have worn a different dress,' he said.

He guided her around the floor with a flourish.

'You had dance lessons, didn't you?'

He smiled. 'I have to admit it. And horseback riding lessons, too. But I'm terrified to get on a horse.'

Despite her resolve she found herself succumbing to the moment. She granted herself permission, as he held her close, to match him step for step, touch for touch.

But then he said, 'What if I want us to go on beyond this evening?'

'You have to listen to me,' she said, her head resting against his shoulder. 'I know you're used to getting what you want.'

'I was until I met you. Now I'm not so sure.'

'Please listen to me now,' she said. 'There are a million women just dying for you to look their way.'

He held her even closer, speaking softly into her ear. 'Is that the truth?'

'The truth,' she said, 'as though you don't know.'

'Yeah? Then why are you making me work so hard?'

'Please . . . don't say that.'

He was about to kiss her, oblivious to all the inquiring eyes staring at them, and she was ready to accept his kiss, when Seigal tapped his shoulder breaking the spell.

'Mind if I cut in?' he said.

Marshall stared at him, his expression grim, and reluctantly released Marisa.

'Congressman Grey would like to continue his conversation with you.' He stepped aside to reveal the congressman smiling broadly and gesturing toward Marshall.

'I'm supposed to be at his beck and call?'

'Go talk to him,' Seigal said. 'Make him happy. That's what this evening is all about.'

'Maybe for you,' Marshall grumbled. 'I'll be right back, Caroline.'

Seigal reached out his arms for Marisa. 'May I?'

'Looks like you already have.'

'Be careful. I've been known to step on toes.'

'That's a coincidence. I've been known to kick shins.'

'Funny.'

They danced for a moment in silence.

'In case we haven't really met, I'm Jerry Seigal,' he said. 'And you're Caroline, right?'

She smiled and looked around. 'Nice party,' she said. 'The rich and the famous. All right up close.'

'Yeah,' he said, regarding her closely. 'You know what my mission in life is?'

'No. What is your mission in life.'

'To take Christopher Marshall all the way to the top.'

'Well, I wish you luck.'

'Tell me something, Caroline. . . .' He waited.

'Well, ask me, Jerry. I can't tell you if you don't ask me.'

'Is there anything I need to know that I don't know already?'

'Such as?'

He shrugged and lurched into her awkwardly. 'Sorry. I'm a klutz.'

'Such as?' she repeated.

'Well . . . anything.'

'I think that's one of those things that's between you and your God.'

'What does that mean?'

'Whatever you want it to mean.'

Seigal gave a brief smile. 'Look – I like a good mystery as much as anyone. But not in his girlfriends.'

'I'm not his girlfriend.'

'Whatever you want to call it. I need him focused tonight.'

Seigal jumped slightly as he felt a tap on his shoulder. Marshall smiled down at him and deftly stepped in, leaving

Seigal to talk to Congressman Grey and Caroline Lane. She had suddenly appeared and was glaring at Marisa.

'Sorry about the interruption,' Marshall said as he steered her into the middle of the floor, away from the others. 'Where were we?'

She smiled. 'You tell me.'

'I think right about here, wasn't it?' He held her close, and again, against her will, she gave in to the pressure of his body. She closed her eyes and for a moment let pure sensation spill over her. When she opened them she saw Seigal in earnest conversation with Maddox and looking her way with a suspicious glance.

'You'd better do what you have to do,' she told Marshall. 'Jerry thinks I'm distracting you by being here.'

'Never, Caroline, *never*, *ever* start a sentence with "Jerry thinks".'

She laughed. When the song ended, the dance floor started to empty, but Marshall and Marisa remained, standing close, staring into each other's eyes.

'Look . . . Chris. You need to do the right thing.'

He slowly smiled and she looked at him questioningly. 'What are you smiling about. Did I say something funny?'

'It's just . . . up until this minute I didn't know what the right thing is. But I do now.'

'You do what? You're talking in riddles.'

'Don't go anywhere,' he said. 'I'll be right back.' He began to walk away.

He headed for Seigal and the Maddox contingent in a leaning-forward, determined stride.

'Chris,' she called after him. 'Wait up. I didn't mean you're doing the wrong thing. . . .'

He held a finger up, as in 'give me a second,' and passed Caroline Lane without acknowledging her. She was studying Marisa, her eyes reduced to slits.

Maybe he knows, Marisa thought, beginning to panic. Or at least suspects something. Why did I ever think it was possible to pull this off? Jesus, get out of here, Marisa Ventura. Move, girl!

She put her head down and walked rapidly past Caroline Lane toward the reception area.

'Excuse me,' Caroline called after her. 'Can I speak to you a minute?'

Marisa was practically running now; she was near the exit when she felt a hand brush her arm. She whirled around to face an out-of-breath Caroline Lane.

'I have the feeling we've met somewhere,' Lane said. 'I'm Caroline Lane. And you are. . . ?'

'Rather in a hurry,' Marisa answered.

Caroline cocked her head, studying Marisa's features. 'I swear we've met. . . .'

Marisa snapped her fingers. 'Wait a minute! Sotheby's Caroline Lane?'

'Why yes!' She beamed at the recognition.

'*Wonderful* to see you again.'

'Then we *do* know each other.' She leaned close to Marisa and fingered her necklace. 'I just *knew* we did. I never forget a face. I have a dim memory of cocktails at the Carlyle, maybe a year, eighteen months ago? That's a Harry Winston Wreath, isn't it?'

Marisa nodded.

'They haven't made that design since the late sixties. Simply ex*quis*ite.'

'You're good,' Marisa said. 'Nothing escapes your eyes. Now if you'll excuse me. . . .'

Caroline put a hand on her sleeve. 'Just between us girls, are you here with Christopher Marshall?'

'Can you keep a secret?'

'Of course.'

'Good,' Marisa said with a bright smile. 'So can I.'

She winked and moved away, leaving a smile frozen on Caroline's features.

Marshall stood with Seigal and Maddox, his eyes roving the room.

'The interview,' Seigal said, nudging him. 'What's your view on that, Chris?'

'Well, you see, Mr Maddox, I appreciate your generosity and your support, but I'm basically a go-it-alone guy.'

'Can a politician ever be that?' Maddox said.

'Chris likes to think so,' Seigal put in. 'All he's really saying is, give him time to work out his priorities.'

'I want an exclusive interview,' Maddox said, turning to Marshall.

'Of course,' Seigal answered quickly. 'We'll effort that.'

'The woman I was dancing with,' Marshall said. 'I need to find her.'

Maddox smiled. 'I like a man who knows what he wants.'

'Good,' Marshall said, giving his hand a quick shake. 'Because what I want just disappeared. Excuse me, won't you?'

As he bolted toward the door, Seigal tried to laugh it away. 'Ah, he's a nut, that Chris Marshall. But a brilliant nut.'

'He seems a bit distracted,' Maddox said, his expression

perplexed. A moment later he moved on, leaving Seigal alone muttering to him. 'Yeah,' he said under his breath, 'a big, stupid, friggin' nut. . . .'

At the top of the steps, in the Plaza fountain area, Marshall caught up with Marisa.

'Do you have someplace else you have to be?'

'No,' she answered. 'I just have to leave.'

'But why? I don't understand.'

'It's complicated.'

'Everything is complicated with you, isn't it?'

'You could say that.'

She started to walk down the steps.

'Well, I'm going to throw this out as a possibility,' he said. 'I don't think you're just leaving. I think you're running.'

Marisa stopped and he walked down past her, blocking her way.

'You do?' she said.

'Yes, running. And what I can't figure out is, are you running toward something you want, in which case go – good luck to you. Or are you running away from something you're afraid you might want?'

She stood in silence as he took her hand.

'Well?' he said.

'You're right,' she whispered. 'I'm running. I'm running from you.'

He nodded and said nothing.

'I've made so many mistakes already. I don't want to make it worse.'

'You won't,' he said. 'I promise.'

'You can't promise that.'

157

He took her in his arms and kissed her. Slowly she returned his kiss.

'Stay,' he said.

'Stay here?'

'No. I mean with me.' He stared into her eyes. 'Stay the night with me. . . .'

14

At one o'clock in the morning, after several hours of talking and intense love-making, Marisa and Chris Marshall lay in bed propped up on pillows, trays of food spread out before them. They were famished; neither of them had eaten since lunch the day before. Marshall forked an oyster from its shell, dipped it in spicy sauce and offered it to her. She opened her mouth but pulled back at the last second.

'First person ever ate one of those must've been either blind or really, really hungry.'

'Close your eyes,' he said.

She did and leaned forward. He tipped the oyster over her lips, she took it in her mouth and swallowed. She smiled without opening her eyes.

He lay back, his hands laced under his head. 'Good, huh?'

'Interesting,' she said. '"Good" might be stretching things. But definitely weird and interesting.'

He traced her features with a finger. 'Well, at least you tried something new.'

'Seems to be my night for it.'

He regarded her seriously, then broke into a big grin. 'Mine too, if you want to know the truth.'

She touched his silken hair and pushed back a lock that had fallen over his eyes. 'Why are you smiling?' she said.

'You could say post-coital content.'

'Well, that's an answer.'

He traced her mouth with a finger. 'I can't believe you're here.'

'Me either. I mean I *shouldn't* be here, in your bed. . . . You know – everything.'

'I didn't mean it that way. I meant I'm happy you're here with me. Can I tell you a secret?'

'Sure.'

'I don't believe I've ever been this happy. You're the reason.'

'But this isn't me. I'm a Catholic, a stickler for doing things the right way. I'm not the kind who just goes to bed. . . .'

He leaned forward and kissed her through her words, and the kiss lingered.

'Or then again, maybe I am,' she said. 'I don't know anymore.'

He kissed her eyelids, her hair, the rims of her ears above the earrings.

'No one's judging you here.'

'Everybody judges.'

'Out there maybe.'

She rolled her eyes. 'You have no idea. Everything you do gets looked at, taken apart. One false move and you're toast. Somebody's gonna condemn you.'

'I know,' he said. 'People have been judging me my whole life. All they see is a photo op, or a candidate, or my father's son. What they don't know is, I was a poor student. I flunked

160

my first year of law school. I thought I wanted to be an artist, not a politician. But I was no Picasso with the paints, not by a long shot – my father, though, he was wonderful, always supporting me, never judging. He got me over the hump and helped me grow up. Confidence came slowly but he stood by me, gave me all the chances I needed. When I stumbled – and I did stumble – he was there to pick me up.' Marshall stared at the ceiling, gathering his thoughts. 'The others – the public – the whole media machine – they have no clue who I am.'

'Maybe we're not so different,' she said.

'Maybe not.'

He continued to rain soft kisses on her face and neck.

'Want to hear something?' she said. Her breathing was shallow, she stretched her neck, accepting his kisses.

'Umm. Tell me.'

'The first time you saw me. . . .' His arms were around her, pulling her close. 'The first time you saw me. . . .' She closed her eyes, lost in the kisses. 'I was . . . I was. . . .'

His lips slid slowly down, feathery kisses just barely touching her skin.

'I was. . . . Oh God, Chris.'

'Mesmerizing,' he said, his voice muffled against her flesh.

'Lost,' she said. 'I was lost.'

When Marisa awoke the following morning she had to concentrate for a moment to remember where she was. She rolled over with a sigh, disentangling herself from Marshall and the twisted sheets. The digital clock on the bedside table flipped to six fifty-nine. She bolted up, fear and guilt knifing through her. She checked him. He was sleeping peacefully. She stared at the far wall and tried to pull her thoughts together. You've gone and really dug yourself a hole this time, girl, and how do you plan to climb out of it? One day you're cleaning the York Suite and the next day you're sleeping in the York Suite with the man you're cleaning for, still playing the lying game, pretending to be someone you're not.

Slowly, quietly, she inched out of bed, found her dress, then shook her head. If she walked out of the York Suite wearing that dress she would walk right into instant disaster. She found a T-shirt of Chris' and sweat pants in the corner, on the floor. The pants were many sizes too large but she held them together with one of his neckties that she found hanging in the closet. She folded her dress carefully, removed a hotel laundry bag from the dresser drawer and stuffed the dress in, along with her shoes. In the bathroom she rinsed her mouth, put toothpaste on her right index finger and rubbed her teeth vigorously. She sponged herself as best as she could with a warm soapy washcloth, then did a quick rearrangement of her wrecked hairdo and wiggled into a pair of hotel-issue slippers. She forced herself to examine her features in the mirror and wasn't happy with what she saw. I look like somebody who just screwed her brains out. Dark circles, blotchy skin, a swollen look. Might as well just wear the Scarlet 'A' and be done with it.

She punched the house phone as she sat on the closed toilet seat.

'Hi, honey,' she whispered. 'Listen, I'm already at work. Abuela will pick you up from Steph's in about thirty minutes. And I should be home by six – OK? Did you and Steph have fun?'

'I beat her six straight games of checkers. Maybe I should have let her win a game.'

'That would've been nice. Is she up?'

'Yeah, making coffee. You want to talk to her?'

'No. I'll see her when she gets in.'

'Did you have fun at the gala?'

'Yes. I'll tell you all about it tonight.'

'Did Chris have a good time?'

'I think so.'

'Steph called you around midnight. I guess she was anxious to hear how it went. But you didn't answer.'

'Fast asleep,' Marisa said. 'Got to go, honey.' She softly hung up.

That's the way it goes, she thought. One lie leads to another, and then another and another, and pretty soon it's hard to separate the truth from the lies.

She peeked out the front door, checking to see if the corridor was clear. She then slipped out and quietly shut the door behind her. Clutching the laundry bag to her side, she stole off down the hall. She padded along silently, at a half trot.

Just as she approached the Park Suite the door swung open and Caroline Lane and her friend Rachel stepped into the corridor in running gear. Marisa froze for a moment, shrinking against the wall.

'So what are you planning to do in Buffalo?' Rachel said.

'Kind of run into him,' Caroline answered. 'He's flying there tomorrow – I got his itinerary from Jerry Seigal. Do you think that's too obvious?'

'Not really. You can pull it off, sweetie.'

Marisa took a deep breath and walked by them, head down.

'Morning,' she mumbled.

'Morning,' Caroline said absently.

Rachel stared after Marisa, who stood at the elevator and pushed the 'down' button.

'Do you see what I see?' she whispered.

'The necklace?'

'Exactly. What maid has a diamond necklace like that?'

'I *know*. And she acted so furtive, didn't she?'

'If I were you, I'd report this right now. Your precious Maria may not be so precious after all.'

Twenty minutes later the two women were standing with John Bextrum, Paula Burns and a rattled Keef in front of his bank of monitors. The air was thick with tension.

'Now you say her name is Maria?'

'Yes,' Caroline answered.

'I never trusted her,' Rachel put in. 'Somewhat pushy and overly assertive.'

Bextrum turned to Paula Burns. 'Do we have anyone named Maria on staff?'

'No,' Paula answered.

'Well, let's see what we can learn from the monitor,' Bextrum said, sounding dubious. 'Keef – run it back please. Anything you have pertaining to the Park Suite and the immediate surroundings.'

'Yes sir.'

The monitor showed grainy black and white footage, sped up, of the comings and goings on the twenty-second floor. Caroline leaned forward, squinting at the screen closely, watching the various maids, butlers and guests pass along in fast forward.

'There!' she screamed in outrage. '*There!* My Dolce coat!'

'I knew it,' Rachel said. 'The little thief!'

The monitor showed Ty, Marisa and Christopher Marshall outside the Park Suite walking to the elevator, Marisa looking glamorous in Caroline's all-white ensemble.

'Jesus *Christ*, I can't believe this,' Caroline steamed. 'Everything I have!'

Bextrum glanced at Paula Burns. 'Marisa,' he said in a soft voice.

She nodded, her mouth an angry snip of wire. 'Marisa. . . .'

'Find her,' Bextrum said, 'and Lionel Bloch, too. Tell them they are to meet us in the Park Suite immediately.'

The monitor followed Ty, Marshall and Marisa as they approached the elevator bank. The two French poodles were there and Bextrum stood next to Marisa shaking hands with Christopher Marshall, nodding his head and grinning.

In his frustration, Bextrum whirled on Keef.

'How could you have missed this?' he demanded.

'I'm sorry, sir.'

On the monitor Bextrum was shaking hands with Marshall.

'You sure do photograph well, Mr Bextrum,' Keef couldn't resist saying.

Bextrum shot him a suspicious glance, then turned and walked quickly away from the security desk, followed by Caroline Lane and Rachel.

Minutes later, Paula Burns opened the door to the Park Suite and Marisa and Lionel entered. Bextrum, Burns, Caroline and Rachel stood in the living room facing them. Their expressions were uniformly grim – like facing a firing squad, Marisa thought.

165

'Lionel,' Bextrum began. 'Marisa. Very serious allegations have been made. . . .'

'Interesting,' Caroline said with the edge of a sneer. 'She told me her name was Maria. Is this woman capable of the truth about anything?'

Sensing there was nothing more to lose, Marisa looked her straight and hard in the eye. 'I thought it would be impolite to correct you.'

'Lovely manners.' Caroline rolled her eyes, looking meaningfully at Bextrum. 'Tell me, did you think it would be impolite to steal my clothing and my date?'

'I didn't steal either of them. The clothes were being returned to—'

Paula Burns cut her off, saying, 'Miss Ventura, Mr Bextrum has spent the last thirty minutes trying to persuade Miss Lane not to press formal charges. I suggest you say as little as possible.'

'We have it all on video,' Caroline said, her expression triumphant. 'There's no way in the world you can lie your way out of this.'

The doorbell rang, and as Paula Burns went to answer it, Bextrum fastened his grim expression on Marisa.

'Was everything returned, Miss Ventura?'

'Yes sir.' Her face felt on fire. She was sick with self-disgust and shame.

Paula Burns re-entered the living room with Jerry Seigal and Chris Marshall. Marshall looked at the gathering, his face slack with bewilderment.

'We've got a tight schedule today,' Seigal announced. 'What's the problem here and what's it got to do with the Assemblyman?'

Marshall frowned as he saw Marisa in her maid's uniform. He glanced at Bextrum as though for an explanation.

Caroline Lane moved to his side and touched his shirt-sleeve. 'Chris – I'm terribly sorry to interrupt your busy morning, but we thought you should know as soon as possible.'

He shook his head, continuing to stare at Marisa. His face was pale, there were dark rings under his eyes and stubble showed on his cheeks. He was feeling the effects of the night before. 'Know what? What's going on?'

'The woman you thought was a guest on this floor is the maid on this floor. It's as simple as that. And, I might add, just as pathetic. I think you should tell him, Marisa.'

'Her name is Caroline,' Marshall said.

'No, darling. That's my name. You just don't understand, do you? This awful woman steals clothes and identities.'

'What the hell's happening here?' he said, raising his voice. He pointed a finger at Marisa. 'Why are you dressed that way?'

'Because she's the maid,' Caroline said. 'Aren't you Maria, Marisa, whatever?'

'What are you saying?' Marshall shrugged her hand off his sleeve and said to Marisa, 'Tell me what she's talking about. Is any of this true?'

Marisa forced herself to look into his eyes. She was afraid of what she would see there, but there was no anger, only complete confusion. She nodded. 'Yeah, it's true. . . .' She then looked away, utterly defeated.

Marshall continued to shake his head. He took two steps toward her, then stopped. 'This can't be true. It just can't be.'

'Jesus Christ,' Seigal exploded. 'The press is gonna have a field day with this.'

Bextrum cleared his throat. 'No reason for the press to find out, Mr Seigal. The Beresford is known for its absolute discretion.'

Marshall continued to stare at Marisa, the reality settling in and hurt filling his eyes. He said, almost in a whisper, 'So everything was a lie.'

'No, not everything.' She slowly shook her head.

'Yes it *was*,' Seigal said dismissively. He turned to Bextrum. 'Now I want to know what measures you're taking to prevent her from speaking to the press.'

Marshall raised a hand to his face as though fending off a blow. 'For Christ's sake, Jerry . . .'

'There could be a smear campaign,' Seigal said. 'Think about it – think with your *mind* for a change. Bigger men have been brought down by less.'

'Let me tell you something, Mr Bextrum,' Caroline said, her voice breaking with emotion, clearly putting on a performance for Marshall. 'This would never happen at the Four Seasons.'

'I assure you, Madame, it has never happened here.' He turned to Lionel, his voice tight with suppressed anger, and said, 'You're slipping, Mr Bloch. You should have noticed something. I'm really terribly disappointed.'

'He had nothing to do with this,' Marisa said. 'Don't blame him.'

'Please, Miss Ventura, I can handle this,' Lionel said. And to Bextrum: 'I understand your position, sir. The incident is most unfortunate for the hotel and I take full responsibility.'

'We'll discuss it later.' He turned his gaze on Marisa. 'As for you, Miss Ventura, you are terminated immediately. Please surrender your passes and ID to security before you leave.'

Marshall moved toward Bextrum. 'Is that really necessary? I'm sure we don't know the entire story.'

'Let the man do his job,' Seigal said. 'Stay out of it.'

With a last look at Marshall – a look he found difficult to decipher, or to forget, combining as it did longing and regret along with an admixture of other emotions – Marisa left the suite.

Following an awkward silence, Caroline said, 'Chris, I can't help but feel this is partly my fault.'

'It isn't,' he said. 'Spare yourself.'

'At least let me buy you lunch,' she said brightly. 'We've only got each other to get through this . . . *humiliation.*'

Marshall's patience with her was exhausted and he made no attempt to hide his feelings. 'Let's get something clear,' he said. 'The first lunch was a mistake. A second would be a complete disaster.'

She smiled ever more brightly, refusing to accept the inevitable. 'Well, drinks then?'

Keef was missing from the security desk. When Marisa asked for him the fill-in security guard said he had gone home early.

'Was he sick?'

'Don't know, Marisa. I was just called down here to take over.' He shot her an embarrassed glance, then quickly looked away.

'This sucks,' he said.

'Don't worry about it, Chet.'

'You're the best. Everybody's gonna miss you.'

'Thanks.'

He started going through her personal effects. 'Sorry,' he said, 'but this is part of the procedure. The tote bag too.'

'It's OK. You gotta do your thing.' As she opened the bag she noticed Lionel behind her, also turning in his ID.

'Oh no,' she said, shocked. 'Please tell me they didn't fire you over this.'

'No, actually they didn't. I made a decision a few moments ago that was long overdue.'

'You mean you quit?'

'Sometimes we're pushed in directions we ought to have found for ourselves.'

'I know,' she said. 'Isn't the word inertia?'

He nodded. 'To serve people takes dignity and intelligence, Miss Ventura. To serve stupid people takes a great deal more of both. But you must keep in mind, they're only people with money. And though we serve them, we are not their servants. What we do can never define who we are. Rather, we are defined by how well we rise after falling. I think you'll make a wonderful manager one day, and it's been my great honor to have worked with you.'

'It's been my honor, too, Mr Bloch.'

They left the service entrance together and Marisa watched the old butler, shoulders back, disappear around the corner.

'Goodbye, Lionel,' she whispered, her eyes filling with tears. 'I'll never forget you . . .'

She clutched her tote bag to her side with one hand and carried her canvas bag with the other and started trudging toward the subway. Halfway down the block, Marshall caught up with her.

'Caroline?' he yelled, and fell in stride beside her. 'Marisa?'

She stopped and turned to him.

'You're crying,' he said.

'Why not? I've got things to cry about.'

'I don't know which name to use.'

'Marisa. Marisa Ventura.'

'What just happened? I don't get it.'

'What don't you get? I'm the maid. I impersonated the woman in the Park Suite, like she said. I stole her clothes and identity.'

'But why? That's not you. I know that's not you. I mean was it some kind of bet? A little game of "let's-get-the-guests?" '

'No,' she said. 'It wasn't like that at all. I tried on her clothes and then you were there with my son and you invited me out, and . . . everything went so fast. A runaway train . . . And I was on it, and there was no way to get off. . . .'

Marshall said, 'And you thought you had to lie to keep me interested?'

Marisa took a step toward him, beginning to show her anger. 'Come on, who's kidding who here? Let's get real. You think you would've taken a second look at me if you knew I was the maid? No way – maids are invisible. They're *supposed* to be invisible. With all due respect for your big-hearted politics, you wouldn't have given me the time of day, Mr Assemblyman.'

'You didn't even give me a chance. How would you know? You stand on your soapbox judging everyone, so sure they're judging you.'

In her agitation she swung her bag, nearly hitting him. 'You think they're not? Well, think again. Half the time I'm some stereotype the guests make jokes about, the rude ones, the noses-in-the-air, if they notice me at all. The other half, I'm invisible.'

'There's that word again. You're stuck on it.'

'But it's true! That's the point of the whole thing. The first time you saw me, I was on my hands and knees cleaning your bathroom floor. Only you didn't see me, did you? Come on, Chris, *did you?* Be honest. . . .'

'What was I supposed to do, introduce myself? I wasn't exactly in a position to start a conversation with you. Jesus, Marisa, you can't nail me for that.'

She looked at him for a long moment and sighed. 'You're right, I can't. OK – you want the truth?'

'I want that more than anything.'

'There was a part of me that was dying to see what it felt like to have someone like you look at *me* like you did. I needed to have that at least once in my life.' Her voice began to break. 'And . . . I'm sorry. I'm truly sorry. If I could rewind the last few days and start over, I would. I've just screwed up things for both of us.'

Seigal rushed up and pushed in between them. 'People, come on. What are you doing, huh? Your little Italian opera here is being photographed by an army of paparazzi.'

'Not now, Jerry. We're in something important here.'

'Yeah, you're selling tickets, for God's sake. You might as well hand out popcorn.'

Marshall noticed a hunched figure scurrying closer between two parked cars, his camera to his eye, looking for a better, closer angle.

'Well, what do you know, it's Yatter,' he said. 'The guy's all over me like a bad rash.'

'You'd better go,' Marisa said.

'I don't care. I don't care what they say, what they do, what they think.'

'You care,' she said quietly.

He reached for her hand. 'Was any of it real, Marisa? I need to know that.'

'Yeah,' she answered, her voice trembling. 'It was real. So real it made me wonder how I could ever give you up. But I have to give you up.' She turned to Seigal. 'Right, Jerry? Isn't that the master plan?'

He threw up his hands in exasperation.

'Can you two end this so we can get out of here?'

'And then last night,' she said, staring into Marshall's eyes, 'I couldn't ... I just couldn't say goodbye. My day with you was over ... but how could I ever let it end?'

15

Marisa could not bring herself to go directly home. She could not face Ty and her mother and have to tell them about her disgrace, her loss of a job she had held proudly for nearly four years. She sat in a swing in an empty graffitied playground in the Bronx and let the tears flow. Rotten luck with men, she thought. I fall for the wrong ones, the ones not meant for me. Marcus and I had nothing in common beyond the sex. He had no interest in improving his mind and moving up in the world. It was all about money and getting enough of it to feel superior to a social world he felt in his bones was superior to him. And Chris . . . Chris is part of that social world that Marcus hates so fiercely, and what do I have in common with him beyond sex? Last night we learned all about the sex. But I am strictly the other side of the tracks. I am a maid and he is a rising political star from a background of education and privilege. Good going, girl. You sure know how to pick 'em.

And worse, you lied to him.

You screwed up big time, Marisa Ventura.

She rocked in the swing and wept.

When she walked into the apartment at eight o'clock, Ty was doing his homework at the kitchen table. Veronica was at the sink washing dishes.

Marisa kissed Ty on the forehead.

'Hi, honey.'

'Hi, Ma.

'What's the homework?'

'Geometry,' he answered. 'I really enjoy working with the points, lines and angles, doing all the measurements. It's sure got algebra beat. Did you know that geometry is the oldest kind of math there is? The Pythagorean Theorem dates back to Babylon, a thousand years before the Greeks. Isn't that cool?'

'That's interesting, baby.'

She dropped her bags on the floor beside the table with a sigh.

'Rosalie from personnel called,' her mother said, her back to Marisa, bent over the sink.

Marisa didn't answer. She pulled up a chair next to Ty and, chin in hand, she watched him work.

'We expected you hours ago,' Veronica said.

'I had things to do.'

Ty looked up. 'Ma – you OK?'

'Sure. Scoot over a little. Let me see if I can understand some of this geometry stuff.'

'I can explain it to you if you want.'

'Isn't geometry ninth grade?'

176

'I'm taking a special course. The school suggested it.'

'You didn't tell me.'

'I started two weeks ago.'

'What about dinner?' Marisa said. 'You hungry?'

'We ate an hour ago,' Veronica said. 'We waited for you an hour.'

'Don't start up, Ma.'

Veronica turned off the faucet and swung around to face Marisa. 'I don't know what to say.'

'Well, then maybe it's better not to say anything.'

'We need to talk, young woman.'

'I'm a grown woman, Veronica Ventura. Your daughter, but all grown up.'

Ty gathered up his books. 'I'm gonna work in my room,' he said. 'It's quieter.' He quickly slipped out.

Veronica studied her daughter, shaking her head. 'Look at me.'

'No. I'm going to take a bath.'

Marisa left the kitchen with her mother a step behind her. She followed Marisa into her bedroom and sat on the edge of the bed as Marisa started to undress.

'Don't, Ma,' she said. 'Whatever it is, I don't want to hear it.'

'What were you thinking? Going out with someone like that. I always gave you credit for more sense, then you go and do something like that.'

Marisa went into the bathroom and turned on the hot and cold faucets in the tub, standing over it until she got the proper mixture. Her mother tagged after her.

'Any soap bubbles?'

'We're out.'

'Damn...' She turned to her mother. 'Something like what?'

'What do you mean?'

'You said I went and did something like that. Like *what*?'

'*Christopher Marshall*,' her mother shouted. 'You had to pretend to be someone else so he would go out with you. That's just pathetic. Where's your pride, Marisa?'

'I see Rosalie didn't spare the details.'

'She told me everything.'

'Good old Rosalie.'

She left the bathroom, tying her robe tight at the waist. 'You're shadowing me, Ma. You're making me nervous.'

'I would like some answers.'

'You know what it is? I think I understand it better than I ever did before. People like you make people like him into Gods, because he's rich and he's white and he's got everything none of us ever had. Everything none of us ever dreamed of having and it must really drive you nuts that I think I have the right to go out with him.'

'You don't have the right.'

'That's the way you see it?'

'It's exactly the way I see it.'

Marisa regarded her mother for a moment and slowly started shaking her head.

'What happened to you, Ma?'

'Excuse me?'

'You're a remarkable woman. You could have been whatever you wanted. What were you so afraid of that made you think you deserved less? What made you just stop trying?'

'Don't speak to me that way, Marisa. A little respect. I'm

not the one who lost her job today.'

Marisa went back into the bathroom to turn off the water.

'No, I did,' she said. 'I really messed up, and I have no one to blame but myself. But it's all right – you know? I'm gonna be fine.'

Veronica nodded. 'Of course you are. Tomorrow we'll call Mrs. Rodriguez. She owes me a favor. She's got a service of maybe ten girls cleaning apartments all over the city. With your experience she'll snap you up, no questions asked. And Marisa, these are good jobs, you know what I'm saying? Nice homes. I'll call her first thing in the morning.'

Marisa brushed a strand of hair away from her mother's forehead. 'Look, Ma, I love you. I really do. But no way I'm going to work for Mrs Rodriguez. I don't want to clean other people's houses. There's nowhere to go from there. I want to work up to hotel management – eventually manage a hotel.'

'Oh sure. That's just great. Lots of people are gonna want to hire you. Just look how good you did at the Beresford.' She closed her eyes and breathed deeply. 'Hasn't this taught you anything? Wake up! You got responsibilities.' She held up a hand, partially closed. 'What do I have here?'

'Nothing that I can see.'

'Imagine it's a fistful of bills. They come every month like clockwork, you know? Lofty dreams don't stop them from coming. You want to be back in the projects? Keep dreaming about things that will never happen and that's where you're gonna be. You want to put food on the table, call Mrs Rodriguez.'

Marisa stared at her mother for a long moment, then said, 'Yeah, you're right, Ma. I'm a good cleaning girl. Never been a dust mouse that could get by me. I'm going to start over.'

Her mother ruffled her hair and gave her an encouraging smile. 'Now you're talking some sense.'

'But not with Mrs Rodriguez,' Marisa continued. 'I'll find a job as a maid in one of the good midtown hotels. And after a while I'll apply to their management training program – and when I get another chance at management, well, I won't screw it up this time.'

Veronica shook her head furiously, refusing to listen.

'And I'm going to make management, Ma. I know I will. And I'll take it on without any fear, without your voice in my head telling me I can't do it.' She stood inches from her mother now. 'Because if I ever let that voice stop me again, I might turn into what I fear most . . . A defeated person . . . A loser.'

'Is that what you think of me?'

She kissed her mother on the cheek. 'Get out of here now,' she said. 'Let me take my bath in peace.'

The following morning Marisa, dressed carefully in a white blouse, a gray skirt and low-heeled black shoes, left her apartment to start job hunting in Manhattan. Stephanie had called to tell her there were openings at the Roosevelt Hotel, and Lionel had called to say that he would write a glowing recommendation for her.

As soon as she opened the front door and stood at the top of the stoop, her hand flew to her mouth, a gesture that would be featured on the front page of the *New York Post* the following morning. She backed up against the door, wanting to bolt back inside, as reporters and photographers swarmed around shooting and shouting questions.

One reporter said, 'Ms Ventura, how did it start? Did Marshall come on to you?'

A photographer started to climb the steps.

Marisa pointed a finger at him and said, 'Don't come any closer. I mean it.'

Another reporter shouted, 'Is it true the Assemblyman didn't know you were a maid?'

'Leave me alone,' she said, her voice growing stronger. 'I have nothing to say. Go away, all of you.'

The first reporter grinned as he said, 'Is it fair to say you could be considered a Beresford perk?'

She glared at him and said nothing.

A young reporter, more intrepid than the others, took the steps two at a time and shoved a copy of the *Post* into her hands, then quickly backed away. She stared at the front page in shock. It featured a photograph of her and Chris in full battle stance, with the headline: DO NOT DISTURB, and bulleted underneath: *Chris Marshall in lover's spat with Beresford chambermaid.*

The young reporter said, 'Marisa – could you hold it up and give us a smile?'

The cameras continued to flash.

She turned and fled back inside.

In Christopher Marshall's office in the Capitol building in Albany, Marshall and his chief of staff sat in front of a large-scale TV watching the Fox news channel's jumpy digital video coverage of the sidewalk set-to the day before.

'Come on, who's kidding who here? Let's get real.' Marisa was saying, the jittery handheld camera capturing her anguish. 'You think you would've taken a second look at me if you knew I was the maid? No way – maids are invisible. They're supposed to be invisible. With all due respect for your big-hearted politics, you wouldn't have given me the time of day, Mr Assemblyman.'

And Marshall was saying, 'You didn't even give me a chance. How would you know? You stand on your soapbox judging everyone, so sure they're judging you. . . .'

Marshall hit the remote and the screen went black. He tossed the remote on the table and buried his head in his hands. 'Jesus, that Yatter. I could cheerfully kill him.'

Seigal paced the floor. 'You're fair game, buddy, don't blame him. He's just doing his job, like you should be doing yours. Working your balls off to get elected. You screwed up big time.'

'Yeah. I screwed up.'

'We gotta make a statement, and the sooner the better. No Clinton cover-up, it all depends on what "I" means or whatever that bullshit was. Just say it straight, but look noble doing it. You can pull it off if anybody can.'

Marshall nodded.

'So what are you gonna say? Pitch me.'

'You want me to spin this, Jerry?'

'Well, what the hell else? We're up to our ass in doo-doo here.'

Marshall suddenly jumped to his feet and raced for the door.

'Chris – *Chris*, what are you doing? Wait up. . . .'

★

The Capitol pressroom was packed with photographers and reporters as Marshall took the podium. He blinked at the flashes but managed to smile and appear calm and statesman like. No one could have possibly guessed that his pulse was humming away at Mach speed and his stomach was tied in knots.

'I would like to make a short statement,' he said, his voice grave but steady. 'And it will be all I have to say about this invasion of privacy. I will take no questions.'

There was a murmur of protest at that, but he raised a hand and smiled. 'This is a statement, people, and not the beginning of a dialogue. OK?' He cleared his throat, sipped water and continued. 'I happened to meet Ms Ventura and her son during my stay at a hotel in New York City. We became friends and we remain friends. My only regret is that Ms Ventura is being subjected to the scrutiny and innuendo of the media as a result of her friendship with me. I wish more than anything that you people would cease and desist. There is no story here beyond a friendship between two people based on mutual respect. Ms Ventura is an inno-cent victim of this unnecessary feeding frenzy. That is all I have to say. Thank you.' He turned and quickly left the podium.

That evening Seigal and Marshall went out for drinks, at Seigal's suggestion. The two men rarely socialized and at first there was a stiffness, a reserve, between them. Marshall ordered scotch on the rocks and Seigal a martini.

'You a martini man, Jerry? I didn't know that.'

'Sometimes. They keep my brain from spinning too fast.' He hesitated, then said, 'You were good today.'

'Thanks. Coming from you that's big news.'

'Straightforward, to the point, no bullshit. You really did yourself proud.'

'Stop it. You'll make me blush.'

Seigal sipped his drink, staring at Marshall over the top of his glass. 'You're really hung up on her. . . .'

'I don't want to talk about it.'

Seigal nodded. 'Fair enough.' After another pause, he said, 'You OK?'

'I'm OK. I'll be fine. What about you?'

'Pumped. We've been through some rough patches, but you're the man, Chris, the golden prospect. Tomorrow you're a candidate, and then, with a little luck and a lot of me, a United States Senator. How's that feel?'

Marshall smiled. 'I can't help thinking about my father.'

'We all miss him,' Seigal said.

'Sometimes I feel that people look at me and expect him. I'm not my father, Jerry. I can't live up to that.'

Seigal sipped his drink and grinned. 'Assemblyman, I knew Grant Marshall. I worked with Grant Marshall. Grant Marshall was a friend of mine. And you, sir, are no Grant Marshall . . .' He reached across the table and clicked Marshall's glass. 'You're better, Chris. For all of your father's good qualities – and he had many – he needed to be liked so much he didn't make the choices that would have made him great. Trust your instincts and stay stubborn.'

Marshall nodded and smiled. 'I'll try my best,' he said.

16

When Marisa began work at the Roosevelt Hotel, she realized with a mixture of amusement and dismay that she had become a minor celebrity. For the first few days as she changed into her uniform other maids would steal glances at her and exchange whispers. One maid, with a thick Eastern European accent, broke the ice by shoving a two-week-old copy of *The New York Post* in front of her with her picture on the front page, along with an open pen. 'You autograph please?'

Marisa shook her head and politely declined.

As the weeks passed the story began to fade and Marisa's natural friendliness won her new work mates over. She missed the daily bantering with friends like Stephanie, Keef and Clarice and made sure to stay in close touch with them. She was overjoyed to hear that Keef had kept his job. She began to regain her emotional equilibrium, and yet Chris Marshall would not go away. He still inhabited her thoughts and dreams. She followed his career closely, searching for news accounts of his doings, and she even attended a rally he gave at a church in Harlem. She sat in the back, near the exit, afraid of being seen. He stood at the podium staring out at an audience that was almost completely Hispanic and black. He had a speech prepared, but as he began to speak he glanced at Jerry Seigal and stuffed the speech in his pocket. He looked out at the audience for a long moment.

'A friend of mine,' he began slowly, 'grew up in the projects. She told me I had no right to speak about life in a place I've never experienced. I think she's right.'

A black woman with a booming voice said, 'What you plan to do, Mr Marshall. Move in with us?'

There was laughter, which Marshall easily joined.

'Maybe,' he said. 'Maybe that's exactly what I should do.'

He turned to Seigal, who was shaking his head no.

'But in the meantime,' he said, 'I'd like to have the people who live here tell me what they think . . . what they need. So I'm turning the meeting over to all of you.' He spread his arms and smiled. 'Talk to me. . . .'

A Hispanic man stood up and said, 'You think a couple of nights living here is gonna tell you anything?'

'No,' Marshall answered. 'But it's a start.'

Slowly hands went up in the multi-racial crowd. Marshall smiled, at ease, fielding the questions and asking questions of his own. What had begun as a speech morphed into a lively town meeting.

Marisa left before the meeting ended.

He's good, she thought. He's learning. And she felt a mixture of pride and longing, an ache deep inside of her.

A week before Christmas Ty sat at the breakfast table reading *The New York Times*. Marisa poured herself a cup of coffee and stared at the small Christmas tree in the living room, its colored lights winking.

Ty looked up and said, 'Today's the nineteenth.'

'Right. Six more shopping days.' She sipped her coffee.

'He's here, Ma. He's back in town.'

'Who? What are you reading?'

'Chris. He's in town.'

Marisa picked up the paper, saw the picture of Chris and put it down. 'So? You going to get dressed? I don't want you late for school again.'

'He's holding a press conference. Did you look at the article?'

'No.'

'Guess where he's giving it.'

'I don't care. Put on your turtleneck. It's cold out.'

Ty took off his pajama tops and pulled the turtleneck over his head.

'At your hotel,' he said. 'The Roosevelt.' He looked at her. 'Ma?'

'What.'

'You listening to me? I said at your hotel.'

'Yeah. I heard you.'

'I mean don't you think that's kind of weird? You'll be there, he'll be there.'

'So will about a thousand other people. I thought we talked about this.'

'I know. But it's like fate.'

'No, it's like New York City and an available conference room.'

Ty stared at her, his grin challenging. 'You knew, didn't you? You weren't going to tell me. You knew he was coming.'

She reached across the table and lifted his chin. 'Honey, remember what we talked about? Huh? He's not a part of our life, but we wish him luck with his. Right?'

Ty nodded. He kicked off his pajama bottoms and put on his pants. He started tying his sneakers, then looked up. 'Ma – you think he misses us?'

'What do you think?'

'I think he does.'

She smiled and ran a hand through his hair.

'He'd be crazy not to,' she said.

She tickled his ribs as they both dissolved into laughter.

At noon the Marshall press conference began in the second floor ballroom at the Roosevelt Hotel. Chris stood in front of a flock of video cameras, reporters and photographers. High level supporters and party officials lined the stage, and as Marshall answered questions Seigal stood by his side.

A reporter from *The Wall Street Journal* said, 'If elected, you'll be the third Marshall to serve New York State. How does that feel?'

'If I get elected,' he said with a slow drawl, 'I'll let you know.'

The response drew a laugh from the press; he was off to a good start.

'Did your father leave you with any advice?' another reporter asked.

'Yeah. He said don't run!'

More laughter; even Seigal grinned widely.

Ty slipped through the door and moved to the center of the press conference, unnoticed.

Fifteen minutes later Marshall was finishing up a question

dealing with commuter taxes, a touchy subject for any New York politico, when Seigal whispered in his ear, 'There's a meet and greet in the Green Room. You OK with that?'

Marshall nodded and turned back to the press.

'We have time for one more question.'

'I have a question,' said a voice. A young voice. A child's voice.

Marshall gripped the podium and strained forward.

'Who's that? I can't see you out there.'

'Hey, Mr Marshall,' shouted a photographer. 'Over here!'

The press parted to reveal Ty in the middle.

Seigal began shaking his head angrily, but Marshall smiled.

'Sure. What's your question?'

The entire room was waiting for the boy to speak. He reached into his pocket and pulled out a paperclip and held it tight in his hand.

'I was wondering . . . I, ah, was wondering. . . .'

He seemed to be losing his nerve and twisted the paperclip in his hand. A bead of sweat broke out on his lip.

Marshall watched and waited. Seigal whispered to him, 'Not now, man. You can't do this.'

'I'm listening,' Marshall said to Ty. 'Go on.'

He swallowed and began again. 'Well . . . I know that everyone makes mistakes. And that it's a sign of character to give a person a second chance, right?'

Marshall nodded. 'Right. I'm with you.'

'Even if someone lied,' Ty continued, 'they should be forgiven. Otherwise we'd never have any Congressmen and Presidents.'

Someone in the audience whistled and there was scattered applause that began to build. Many of the cameras were now

189

trained on the boy as Seigal stepped to the mike.

'Thank you, son. We've got to wrap this up.'

'Wait, he's not done,' Marshall said. 'Go ahead.'

'Well ... What if you're not a politician trying to do good for everybody. What if you're just a regular person ... like a ... like a maid or somebody.'

'Damn it,' Seigal said as the press started to murmur. More cameras turned their eyes on Ty.

'And ... and she made a mistake. Do you think she should get a second chance? I mean nobody's perfect, right?' He clutched the paperclip, his knuckles white with strain.

Marshall nodded. He slowly started to smile.

'No – nobody's perfect. You're right. Ladies and gentlemen of the press, take a look. Take a good look ... at a future candidate.'

The room broke out in laughter and applause. Seigal stepped to the podium and said, 'Thank you all. We'll see you in Buffalo.'

Marshall stepped off the stage accompanied by Seigal, who tried to steer him in the direction of the Green Room, but Marshall shrugged his arm away and headed toward Ty.

'You're throwing it all away,' Seigal hissed. 'You know that, don't you?'

'I'm just trusting my instincts, Jerry.'

They stared at each other for a moment until Seigal shrugged and backed away.

Marshall put a hand on Ty's shoulder. 'Nice speech,' he said.

'Really?'

Photographers surrounded them. Flashbulbs went off.

'You had them eating out of your hands.'

Ty looked at the paperclip, then at Marshall. 'Thanks.'

'No problem.'

They held each other's stare for a moment until Marshall said, 'Where is she?'

The cameras and the reporters followed behind as the man and the boy went in search of Marisa. Seigal trotted along only steps behind.

A reporter said, 'We haven't had a story like this for a while.'

'No comment,' Seigal said.

'It's gonna kill his career.'

'You crazy?' said another reporter. 'The Latin vote alone will put him over the top.'

Seigal brightened as he said, 'He always cared about the Latin people. His whole family did. You can quote me.'

Leading the parade of press, Ty and Marshall walked down a long corridor and entered the hotel cafeteria. Marshall spotted her about to enter the lunch line.

'Marisa?'

She turned and gave a gasp. 'Chris ... Ty ... Why aren't you in school? What's going on?'

Reporters and photographers pressed close. Flashes went off, reporters shouted questions. Marisa looked terrified as she gaped at Marshall.

'I've got nothing to hide,' he said. 'Do you?'

They stared into each other's eyes with a thousand questions. He took her by the hand and walked her out of earshot of the prying eyes and ears.

Seigal held up both hands. 'Breathing space, people. Give them a minute alone.'

'How you doing?' Marshall said.

'OK.' She tried to smile. 'You know.'

He nodded. 'I know. I've been worried about you.'

'I'm fine. I don't . . . need rescuing.'

'I don't want to rescue you, Marisa. I just want . . . a second date. A second chance. You as you, me as me. No secrets. That's all.'

Her expression softened. 'That's all?'

'I don't know. Maybe that's all and maybe it's just the start. But there's only one way to find out, right?'

'Yeah, right.'

She extended her hand. 'OK – let's start out right. Marisa Ventura, housekeeping.'

'Chris Marshall, candidate for the US Senate. I'd appreciate your vote.'

She stared at him for a long moment as they shook hands. 'We'll see,' she said.

Ty watched them as they fell into a long embrace.

'Yes,' he said, gripping the paperclip. '*Yes! Yes!*'